BRANCH

#19829
BL 4.6 PTS 10

DATE DUE		

Circle of Love

Circle
of Love

Joan Lowery Nixon

Delacorte Press

Published by
Delacorte Press
Bantam Doubleday Dell Publishing Group, Inc.
1540 Broadway
New York, New York 10036

Library of Congress Cataloging-in-Publication Data

Nixon, Joan Lowery.
Circle of love / by Joan Lowery Nixon.
p.   cm. — (The Orphan train adventures)
Summary: Nineteen-year-old Frances Mary Kelly, herself an orphan
train rider six years before, returns to New York and agrees to escort
a group of orphans west to find new homes.
ISBN 0-385-32280-1 (alk. paper)
[1. Orphan trains—Fiction.   2. Orphans—Fiction.]   I. Title.
II. Series: Nixon, Joan Lowery.   Orphan train adventures.
PZ7.N65Ci   1997
[Fic]—dc20   96-44950   CIP   AC

The text of this book is set in 11-point Century Schoolbook.
Manufactured in the United States of America
March 1997
10 9 8 7 6 5 4 3 2 1
BVG

A Note from the Author

During the years from 1854 to 1929, the Children's Aid Society, founded by Charles Loring Brace, sent more than 100,000 children on orphan trains from the slums of New York City to new homes in the West. This placing-out program was so successful that other groups, such as the New York Foundling Hospital, followed the example.

The Orphan Train Adventures were inspired by the true stories of these children; but the characters in the series, their adventures, and the dates of their arrival are entirely fictional. We chose St. Joseph, Missouri, between the years 1860 and 1880 as our setting in order to place our characters in one of the most exciting periods of American history. As for the historical figures who enter these stories—they very well could have been at the places described at the proper times to touch the lives of the children who came west on the orphan trains.

Joan Lowery Nixon

CHILDREN
Without Homes.

A number of the CHILDREN brought from
NEW YORK are still without homes.

FRIENDS FROM THE COUNTRY PLEASE

CALL AND SEE THEM.

MERCHANTS, FARMERS
AND FRIENDS GENERALLY

Are requested to give publicity to the above

AND MUCH OBLIGE

H. FRIEDGEN, Agent.

1

JENNIFER COLLINS SETTLED into the plump cushions that lined her wicker chair as Grandma Briley began to read from Frances Mary Kelly's faded blue journal.

Jennifer's brother, Jeff, who had been lying on the floor, propped himself up, chin resting on his hands, and interrupted Grandma. "Wait a minute. You just said that the date of this story was July 1866. Was the Civil War over then?"

"Officially." Grandma brushed a damp strand of gray hair back from her face and took a sip of iced tea. "General Robert E. Lee surrendered the Army of Northern Virginia to General Ulysses S. Grant in April of 1865. That brought an end to the War Between the States."

Jennifer did some quick mental arithmetic. "Frances was thirteen when the Kelly children were sent west by the Children's Aid Society. That was in 1860. So in July 1866, Frances Mary would have been nineteen."

"That's right."

Jennifer sighed. "I remember that when you first began to read Frances's entries, she said her dearest love had given her this journal and told her to write her stories in it."

"If this is a love story, I don't want to hear it," Jeff said, and made a face.

Grandma's eyes twinkled. "There's been love in every story Frances Mary has told. There are many kinds of love! I'm going to read about love, and then you're going to hear a surprising story of adventure and danger. I just said that the war was *officially* over. It had a terrible effect upon some people's hearts and minds. The wounds took a long time to heal."

"Whose hearts and minds?" Jeff asked.

"Oh, be quiet, Jeff," Jennifer said impatiently. "Let Grandma read so we can hear what happened."

Grandma smiled and began with Frances Mary's own words:

Early this morning, I brushed my hair in pale sunlight. As I tucked two silver-edged combs into my hair, I remembered my nineteenth birthday, when Johnny Mueller gave them to me.

And gave me this journal.

"Write the stories you have been carrying in your heart," he said. "Begin with your family. Begin when you were very young in New York. Begin with your own story."

I did. I wrote about my parents and my brothers and my sisters, who meant so much to me.

The words and tears and love spilled out together, capturing our stories forever on these pages.

By this time I should have written about the one I love most of all—Johnny. I should have written about our wedding day—a day of dreams come true. Sadly, though, there has been no wedding.

I'm sure that I loved Johnny from the moment I first met him, when I came to Kansas on an orphan train. I have always known that Johnny loved me. During the war I kept up my spirits by reminding myself that as soon as Johnny returned from his service with the Union Army, we'd marry. But Johnny's one-year internment in a Confederate prisoner-of-war camp took its toll on his health.

Under the strong Kansas sunlight his face has regained most of its color, and his cough no longer shakes his entire body. But the farmwork he once did with strength and ease exhausts him, and the dark depths of his eyes seem to mirror horrors that haunt him like demons.

Since I'm a woman, it would be unseemingly of me to propose marriage, but I have hinted at it in many ways. Each time, Johnny's mouth tightens. He absolutely refuses to talk about marriage.

Over and over I have asked myself: Can't he see what a good wife I'd make? Doesn't he want to know the joys of raising a family together?

It has been a week since I laid down my pen. Tears came to my eyes as I reread what I wrote about Johnny and the questions I asked myself. If I had known the answers, perhaps I would never *have let my temper run away with me. Johnny and I wouldn't have had such a terrible argument on our way to town, and I wouldn't have plunged into a sudden course of action that changed my entire life.*

2

FRANCES MARY KELLY rode on the front seat of the Muellers' wagon next to Johnny. Hot July air from the Kansas prairie, fragrant with the sharp scent of newly cut grasses and freshly turned earth, swirled around them. Plowed ridges lay to their right, grazing land to their left. In the distance a snaking line of scrubby trees marked the presence of a stream, and close to the stream stood a house.

The door opened and Frances caught a flash of blue. She knew the woman who wore the blue dress—Elvira Reading.

"El-mer! Come right this minute!" The high and low notes in the woman's voice carried through the stillness, as did the voice of the child who answered, "Coming, Ma!"

Frances held a hand to her chest, pressing against

a growing ache. *That is what I want for Johnny and me*, she thought. *Marriage, a home, children. Why can't it be?*

She slid a little closer to Johnny on the wagon seat, glancing at his broad shoulders, at the way his sun-bleached hair curled under the snug leather band of his hat, and at his hands firm on the reins.

Frances had met Johnny on the day the Cummingses had brought her to Kansas. The Mueller family, along with other near neighbors, had come to share the Cummingses' joy at having adopted two orphan train children. That night, while she thought the other children were sleeping—all of them on pallets in front of the fireplace—Frances had given in to a desperate loneliness for her mother and brothers and sisters and cried.

Johnny had been awake and had heard her, but he hadn't teased. Keeping his voice low so as not to wake the others, he'd whispered, "Ma said you had to leave your other brothers and sisters. If I had to leave Matt and Karl and even old froggy Fred over there, I'd cry, too." Maybe—just maybe, Frances thought, she had begun to fall in love with Johnny's good humor and kindness and understanding at that moment.

Aware of her gaze, Johnny looked down at Frances. Their eyes met.

"I see that the Readings have finished their new house," Frances said. "They've moved out of the soddy."

Johnny looked back at the road without answering, but Frances plunged on. "Elvira worked on that house along with her husband. She could pound a nail and use a saw as well as Harry could. Elvira told me that—"

"Harry didn't serve in the army," Johnny said. "He wasn't in a Confederate prison."

"What has that got to do with—?"

"He wasn't injured. He wasn't starved. He's perfectly fit for a man's work, yet he chooses to accept a woman's help. It's not something I would do."

Frances choked down the anger that rose in her throat and slid a little farther away from Johnny. "Perhaps Harry sees a husband and wife as a team, willing to work together at whatever job needs to be done. Perhaps he isn't as . . . as . . . stubborn as you." The word was out before she could stop it.

"You think I'm stubborn, do you?" Johnny gave a quick flick to the reins, and the plodding horses picked up their pace. "Oh, Frances, I know it's hard for you to understand, but it was that stubbornness—as you put it—that kept me alive in the Confederate prison. I refused to give in to the maggots crawling through the food, to the freezing rain that soaked to the bone, and to the stench of illness and death around me. I refused to give up and die with so many members of my company." He hesitated. "Although I . . ."

"You have to stop feeling guilty about their deaths," Frances said. "You were not to blame. Your company was outnumbered and captured."

"But my friends died, and I was spared. Why? Tell me why." Before she could speak he shook his head and said, "I have searched for an answer, and there is none."

Frances took a long, steadying breath. "I know it was hard, Johnny. I prayed for you. I ached for you. I cried for you. And when you came home to your parents, I did everything I could to help you."

"I know, and I'm grateful," Johnny said. He took Frances's hand and held it gently. "I understood that I couldn't have survived without you."

Frances was determined to continue. "But that horrible time in your life is over now, Johnny. Your body is healing, yet you refuse to put your year in prison out of mind." Tears burned her eyes as she remembered Johnny's ready smile and eager laughter, which she'd rarely seen or heard since his return.

"It's impossible to put it out of mind. I'll never forget. Never."

"Please don't dwell on the past," Frances said. "Look forward. Think of the happiness that lies ahead. Think of the happiness we can share."

Johnny sighed, and for a moment his broad shoulders sagged. "I'm sorry, Frances. I don't want to talk about marriage. It's not time to even think of marriage."

Her spine stiffened, and she flung her words at him. "Why? Because you didn't come back from the war the same as when you left home? Do you think that would make me love you any the less?"

Rising on the horizon ahead of them Frances could see the row of one- and two-story wooden buildings that made up the town of Maxville. Could she convince Johnny before they arrived?

"You don't understand," Johnny mumbled.

"I *do* understand."

For just a moment Johnny's face softened as he turned to her. "Frances, someday you and I . . . and our children . . ."

"Someday?" Frances asked. "Why not *now*?"

She raised one hand, reaching out to him, but

Johnny's jaw clenched and the closed, stubborn look came into his eyes again. "Not until I'm able to work my land again without help."

"We can work together."

"I will not have my wife add to her chores by having to do *my* job."

Frustration turned to anger as Frances blurted out, "Wife? What wife? If you insist on waiting for everything in the whole world to be perfect, you'll never have a wife!"

Johnny groaned. "Frances, why are you doing this to us?"

"Me? You're blaming me?"

"Of course I'm blaming you. If you could just try to be patient—"

Furious at Johnny and at the Irish temper that had got the best of her, Frances snapped, "I'm sorry, but I'm fresh out of patience. You either love me as I am, the way I love you, or look elsewhere for a suitable wife."

"Frances . . ."

"There's nothing more to say." Choking back tears, Frances turned away from him.

As soon as they reached the main street of Maxville and Johnny had pulled the horses up beside the uneven wooden sidewalk, Frances jumped down from the wagon.

"Buy the supplies you need, but leave them with Mr. Nash. When I finish my business at the bank, I'll come to the general store and load them into the wagon," Johnny told her.

Frances didn't answer. Silently fuming, she strode down the sidewalk toward the general store.

Ahead, near the store's entrance, she saw Mrs.

Garrett and Mrs. St. John—two of the liveliest gossips in the area. They had to have noted her arrival in town with Johnny.

Frances realized that her cheeks were flushed and hot and her breathing was rapid. She couldn't greet the women with angry smoke practically pouring out of her ears. Who knew what wild rumors might start?

Frances stopped outside the meeting hall, trying to calm down while she pretended to be very much interested in the poster outside the open doorway.

As she read the words on the poster, she sucked in her breath.

**Come Today.
Meet the Children
From New York City
In Need of Homes.**

There was more, but Frances's eye was immediately caught by the last line on the poster: *Andrew MacNair, Agent.*

"Andrew!" she whispered. She picked up her skirts and flew up the steps into the nearly empty meeting hall.

"Andrew!" she cried, running into the arms of the tall, muscular man, who grinned at her with delight.

The words tumbled out. "There's so much to ask," Frances said. "How is Katherine? I'm so glad I was able to come to your wedding. She was a beautiful bride. And you, Andrew—you're looking well. Have you seen Ma lately? Since Danny's death the heart seems to have gone out of her. Her letters—"

She suddenly stopped. "I'm babbling on, aren't I? But there's so much to say."

Placing his hands on Frances's shoulders, Andrew

answered, "Katherine is fine, and so is your mother. Now, tell me. How is Frances Mary Kelly? And Johnny? Did he come to town with you?"

Frances shrugged and tried to smile again. She didn't want Andrew, or anyone else, to discover how hurt and angry Johnny had made her. "Johnny's health is improving rapidly," she said. "As for me, school is out for the next two months, but I've been allowed to remain living in the teacher's house. I plan to study, tutor a few students, and hire out to help some of the farm wives with summer chores."

Andrew's smile broadened. "Then you're not committed to something you can't leave for a while. It's just as I had hoped. Would there be any problems if you were out of town for a few weeks?"

"Out of town? Where?"

"I was going to call on you this afternoon," Andrew said. "I have a favor to ask of you."

"A favor that would send me away from Maxville?" Frances smiled. "Don't be so mysterious, Andrew. Tell me what the favor is."

"It's a boy. His name is Stefan Gromeche." Andrew turned and called, "Stefan? Will you come here, please? There is someone I want you to meet."

From the shadows at one corner of the room stepped a scrawny boy, about ten years old. His cap was pulled low over a ragged haircut, and the suit he'd been given seemed a size too large.

"Hello, Stefan," Frances said. She held out a hand.

Stefan shook her hand and smiled. "I'm going home," he said.

"Home?" Frances looked at Andrew for an explanation.

"Stefan's parents died, and he was brought to the Children's Aid Society," Andrew said. "After he left

11

with us on the train, an aunt and uncle came to the Society's office. They had just arrived in the United States, and they asked us to return Stefan to them."

"Good. He'll have family," Frances answered. She well remembered the fear, heartache, and uncertainty she had felt as an orphan train rider. She had traveled with her brothers and sisters on the orphan trains six years ago, but it almost seemed as though it had happened yesterday. "Now you'll be going back to New York City with Andrew," she said to Stefan, "to join your aunt and uncle."

Stefan beamed. Andrew spoke up. "Not exactly," he said. "This is the favor I want to ask of you, Frances. I have business dealings that must be taken care of. I have no choice. Would it be possible for you to escort Stefan to New York?"

Flustered, Frances said, "Oh, no. I—I couldn't."

"Please, Frances, think about it. School is out. You won't have children to teach for the next few weeks." Andrew reached into the inside pocket of his coat and pulled out two train tickets.

"But I have duties," Frances said. "Granted, they're not urgent, but even so . . . How long do I have to decide?"

"I need to know today. If you can't help me out, I'll have to find someone else." Andrew held up the tickets and said, "The train leaves tomorrow. Your ticket is round-trip. You'll spend two nights under the care of Miss Claudine Hunter, who works at the Society's office, then return to Kansas. And just think, you'll have enough time to see some of New York City again."

Frances's heart gave a thump. New York City! The

very name made her feel thirteen years old once more. Suddenly every facet of the city came vividly alive in her memory. She could almost see the bustle of people, hear the shouts of drivers from the crowded cabs and wagons, smell the salt air and the horse droppings and the overperfumed ladies on the avenue. And she could feel the warmth of the one-room home in which the Kellys had lived. Sometimes they'd been a little hungry, sometimes a little cold, but the strength and comfort of their love had overcome most of their troubles.

A deep longing swept through Frances. She ached to see once more the room where she'd happily sewn piecework with Ma, where Da had been a strong, laughing father before he sickened and died, where Mike and Danny had played and wrestled, where Megan—loving Megan—had cared for little Peg and Danny. She could hear Da's laughter and Mike's banter. She could see Peg twirling on one foot and demanding, "Dance with me, Frances." She closed her eyes as memories swirled into her mind, pulling at her, tugging at her, begging her to come.

Frances had never imagined she'd see New York City again, but Andrew was offering her the chance to go. *I want to go*, she thought. *I have to go!*

But if she went to New York City and back, she'd be away from Johnny for nearly three weeks! She couldn't do it.

"Frances, if I could have your answer by—let's say noon?" Andrew asked.

I'd also be away from the wall of bitterness Johnny is building around himself, Frances thought. *I'd have time to think about what I want to do with my own life, if Johnny doesn't want me.*

13

Maybe this was meant to be so that I'll have the good sense to plan a future without Johnny in it.

Shaken, she raised her eyes to Andrew's. "I can give you an answer now," she said. "I'll take Stefan back to New York."

3

WITH STEFAN TROTTING at her side, Frances tucked his cardboard box from the Children's Aid Society into the wagon. She was familiar with the contents of those boxes—a change of clothing and whatever small family keepsakes, trinkets, or toys the child held dear.

"I think I remember my aunt and uncle," Stefan said. "When I say my uncle's name to myself I see a big mustache. It's thick and wide, like a hairbrush."

Frances chuckled as she led Stefan into the general store. She smiled and nodded at Mrs. Garrett and Mrs. St. John, who stood near the doorway.

Mrs. Garrett's eyebrows rose and fluttered. "Don't tell me you've taken an orphan train child, Miss Kelly. Isn't there some rule against single parents? Or perhaps you and Johnny Mueller have finally decided—"

Frances interrupted. "This is Stefan Gromeche. I'll be taking him back to New York. He has an aunt and uncle waiting for him."

Mrs. St. John giggled and said to her friend, "You're speaking out of turn, Mrs. Garrett, about Frances and Johnny. We haven't been hearing the sound of wedding bells, have we?"

"Please excuse me," Frances said calmly, although she knew her face was burning. Taking Stefan's hand, she pushed past the women and strode into the cool dimness of the store.

Stefan gasped, jerking Frances to a stop. She glanced down at him in surprise. He was staring fixedly at the mounds of fresh carrots, golden onions, and white turnips tinged with purple.

"What are those?" Stefan asked.

Mr. Nash picked up a carrot, rubbed some specks of dirt from it onto his already soiled apron, and handed it to Stefan. "Have you ever eaten a carrot?" he asked.

Stefan shook his head. "At home we mostly had potatoes and cabbage. Then at the orphanage we had bread and butter and sometimes a thick, brown soup." He studied the carrot, then took a bite, jumping as it cracked under his teeth.

"Like it?" Frances asked.

Stefan munched happily. "It's good!"

"So are peppermint sticks," Mr. Nash said. From a jar on the counter he produced a small sugary stick covered with red and white stripes and handed it to Stefan.

"Now, let's fill your order, Miss Kelly," Mr. Nash said. "What's first on the list?"

Frances blinked. "I had a list," she said, "but my plans have changed. I've agreed to escort Stefan to

New York City to meet his aunt and uncle, so I won't need to stock up on supplies." She thought a moment. "I'll just get something to cook for supper tonight and breakfast tomorrow. Carrots, of course, and a fryer. . . . We can take the leftovers on our trip. . . . Oh, and a small jar of molasses. I think Stefan will like flapjacks." She came up with half a dozen items and Mr. Nash fit all her purchases into a string bag.

"I'll put it on your account," he said. "Have a good trip, Miss Kelly, and a safe return."

"Thank you, Mr. Nash." The parcel wasn't heavy, so Frances picked it up and led Stefan out of the store and down the sidewalk to where Johnny's wagon was hitched.

As she pulled two carrots from her bag and handed them to Stefan, showing him how to offer them to the horses, she heard Johnny's voice behind her. "Well, well, who's this fine young man who's giving a treat to my horses?"

Frances turned to face Johnny, but he didn't look at her. He kept his eyes on Stefan.

"Johnny Mueller, this is Stefan Gromeche," she said. "Stefan came to Maxville with the orphan train riders."

This time Johnny did look at Frances, with surprise. "He's an orphan train rider? Then where is . . ." He straightened and glanced around.

"Stefan's aunt and uncle recently arrived in the United States. When they found he'd been sent west on one of the orphan trains, they asked that he be returned."

"My uncle has a *huge* mustache," Stefan said. He spread his hands two feet apart. "It's this big."

"My, my, that's very impressive. I'm glad you have

a fine uncle like that to claim you," Johnny said. He smiled at Stefan. "Would you like to pet my horses? Here . . . I'll hold you up."

This was the Johnny Frances had known, the Johnny with whom she'd fallen in love. Smiling, she watched him reach out to Stefan. Johnny was kind, gentle, and playful, and Frances loved him all the more.

But in a few minutes Johnny said, "It's getting late, Frances. Find the people who are to take care of Stefan, and I'll get your boxes of supplies from the store."

"The only supplies I bought are already in the wagon," Frances said.

He looked surprised. "But you told me you needed to buy a great many things."

Frances pointed to the string sack. "This is all I'll need. I don't want bugs to get into my flour or ants into the syrup while I'm away." She looked at Johnny without smiling and said, "I agreed to escort Stefan back to New York City. If you'll please lift him into the wagon, we can be on our way."

Johnny, unable to move, stared at her. "You're going to New York?"

"Yes. I'll be gone close to three weeks." She added, not knowing why, "Longer, if I decide to stay awhile."

Stefan, too impatient to wait for Johnny to help him, clambered up the spokes of the nearest wagon wheel and into the bed of the wagon. He squirmed like a puppy among some empty feed sacks, finding a comfortable place in which to settle down.

"Frances," Johnny asked, "where will you stay while you're in the city? Who will look out for you?"

She could hear the shock and hurt in his voice.

She wanted to hold him and cling to him, but anger kept her backbone as stiff as the whalebones in her corset. "A Miss Claudine Hunter, from the Children's Aid Society, will meet us at the station and reunite Stefan with his aunt and uncle. And, in case you haven't noticed, I'm perfectly well able to take care of myself!"

"But the church social . . . It's Sunday. . . . We've always gone together. . . ."

"I'm sorry," Frances said. "I promised Andrew that I would take Stefan to his family." As she climbed up on the seat of the wagon she added, "Besides, you didn't ask me to go with you to the church social."

"But . . . but we've always gone together. I didn't think . . ."

Frances held her tongue, although she wished she could say, *You took it for granted that I'd go with you. You take me for granted. You think that I'll tag around after you forever, without a commitment, without a promise, without even wanting to discuss the possibility of marriage. Well, I won't!*

Johnny frowned. "You made the decision to go to New York without talking it over with me."

"There was no need to talk to you," she said. "What I decide to do with my life is up to me and, apparently, no concern of yours."

Fumbling with the reins as he climbed into the wagon, Johnny looked at Frances with stricken eyes. "It *is* my concern. You're a part of my life, Frances," he said.

"But not as much a part of it as the bitterness and anger inside you," she said. "It's like a mean, vicious animal that bites and hurts. But you hug it to yourself and won't give it up. You can't have it and me, too."

"Nonsense! You're talking rubbish," Johnny grumbled.

"Am I?" Frances asked. "Then let's not talk at all."

Silently, they rode a mile out of Maxville to the cleared acre on which the local school and teacher's house had been built.

As they pulled into the yard Johnny said, "I'll take you and Stefan to the train. When do—"

Frances interrupted. "There's no need to. Andrew has arranged to pick us up tomorrow."

"Tomorrow? So soon? And you have no idea when you will be back?"

Frances paused, so sick at heart it was difficult to climb down from the wagon. Softly she answered, "At this moment I just don't know."

She woke Stefan and led him into her house. She settled him into an armchair with an illustrated fourth-grade reader. Then she closed the curtain over the door of her tiny bedroom, which was scarcely large enough for a narrow bed and dresser, and changed clothes. She began a fire in the stove, adding chunks of wood until it was blazing. Next she put floured pieces of chicken into a pan to brown and simmer.

When she saw that Stefan was engrossed in the reader, Frances slipped from the house and ran to the far side of the school. There she dropped onto a bench, rested her head in her hands, and sobbed.

The next morning, on the buggy drive to Maxville's railway station, Frances found it hard to chat with Andrew. She let Stefan babble on about the train, the upcoming trip, and his uncle's gigantic mustache.

She searched the horizon for signs of a rider. Surely Johnny would come to say goodbye. Wouldn't he? Cold fingers clutched her stomach as she wondered over and over whether she had made the wrong decision. She had hoped for so long that Johnny would listen to her and let go of the bitterness he felt toward his Confederate captors. But the bitterness was spreading like a sickness, affecting every part of his life and his future—*their* future together.

Together? No. The angry words she had spoken had brought their togetherness to an end. If only Johnny had stopped her and promised to put away the past and think about the future. If only he'd said . . .

"What do you hear from Megan?" Andrew asked, jolting Frances away from her thoughts.

"Megan writes about little else than the son of one of the Browders' near neighbors," Frances said. "His name is Stuart Wallace, and everything about him is perfect—according to Megan." Frances couldn't help smiling with joy for her sister as she said, "I imagine a wedding date will be set within the year."

"And how is little Petey? He must be growing up fast."

"He's no longer *little* Petey. He's twelve now, and he insists on being called Pete. He's tall and strong and has a real love of farming. From the time we first came to live with the Cummingses, he followed Mr. Cummings around like a puppy. If only he applied himself that well in school." Frances sighed. "It's hard to be Pete's sister and teacher at the same time."

As they reached the outskirts of Maxville, Andrew said, "We see Peg often, since she lives in St. Joe. She mentioned a few months ago that Mike had gone west, looking for gold. Has he had any success?"

"No," Frances answered, "but that doesn't discourage Mike. He tried Colorado and he's in California now." She paused. "Sometimes I think that if Mike were a bird, he'd be an eagle. He soars high, ranges wide, and isn't afraid to tackle anything. Each day of life seems to excite him—even more than the possibility of finding gold."

"At least he's had no more misadventures," Andrew said.

"Oh, I didn't say that!" Frances shook her head. "In Colorado Mike had a run-in with claim jumpers who nearly cost him his life, and in California—"

"There's the train!" Stefan bounced up and down on the buggy seat and shouted in Andrew's ear. "Hurry! We don't want to miss it!"

Andrew hitched the buggy to a post near the depot and carried Frances's carpetbag and Stefan's box to one of the coach cars.

Frances hopefully searched the platform for Johnny, sick at heart that he hadn't come. Delaying until the conductor shouted, "All aboard!", she mounted the steps to the railway car and hurried to the seats Andrew and Stefan had picked out. She shook hands with Andrew and thanked him for the money he'd given her for traveling expenses.

Andrew said, "I'll wait on the platform until the train leaves. Is there anything else you need?"

I need Johnny, Frances thought, but she shook her head and answered, "I can't think of anything."

She made sure that Stefan was comfortable next to the window, then sat beside him, twisting to see out of the windows on both sides of the car. To her dismay, there was still no sign of Johnny.

It wasn't until the engineer blasted the air with his horn and the chugging engine picked up steam, tugging the string of railway cars faster and faster out of Maxville, that Frances admitted to herself that Johnny wouldn't come to say goodbye.

I'm going to New York, she told herself. The memories and anticipation welled up in her, mingling with her loneliness for Johnny and making it hard to breathe.

The train jerked and swayed. She struggled to put Johnny out of her mind so that she could concentrate on giving Stefan a pleasant trip. She told him stories, explored the train with him, soothed him to sleep with his head on her lap, and fed him fresh milk and apples, meat, bread, and cheese at some of the depot stops along the way.

On the platforms around these depots, she often saw men wearing tattered remnants of army uniforms—both blue and gray.

"They're late in making their way home," she said to the conductor.

He shook his head sadly as he answered, "Some of them no longer have homes, so they're goin' to wander and keep wanderin', I suppose."

"But the war has been over for more than a year."

"Depends on where you live," he said. "I heard that down in Texas they're still fightin'."

Frances shuddered. It was impossible to believe the hatred and cruelty caused by war. But she knew it existed. She'd seen its dark reflection in Mike's and Johnny's eyes.

She had brought her journal, the one Johnny had given her; it helped to record her thoughts and feelings and the descriptions of what she saw and wanted to remember. Putting the story on paper softened the words that burned in her heart and made her separation from Johnny easier to bear.

23

* * *

On the day they were scheduled to arrive in New Jersey, Stefan was so excited that Frances could hardly keep him in hand. He ran from one end of the car to the other, staring out the windows, searching for the tightly clustered buildings that would mean he would soon be greeting his aunt and uncle. Frances was excited, too, and a little fearful. The Kelly family's life in New York City was far in the past. Would returning to the people and places she'd known be too painful?

The train pulled into a large shed, which was crowded with travelers, peddlers, and people who eagerly searched the windows of each car for the faces of those they had come to meet. Now and then someone would spot a loved one and begin shrieking and waving.

Frances wrote in her journal:

> *There seem to be more former soldiers at this station than at any of the others. Remnants of blue mingle with tattered gray without incident. Eyes are downcast or exhausted, no longer sparking with the battlefield's fear and anger. I hope and pray that these weary men are able to forgive and forget and will soon begin to build new lives for themselves.*

One of the men glanced up at Frances. Their eyes met, and he smiled. Remembering the drawn expression on Johnny's face when he returned from the prison camp, Frances gave no thought to proper behavior and smiled back.

Stefan tugged on her arm. "There are my aunt and

uncle! See? They're waving at me! I was afraid I wouldn't remember them, but I do! I do!"

Frances leaned over Stefan's shoulder and looked where he was pointing. A short, slender couple had spotted Stefan. The woman was crying and smiling at the same time. The man looked very much like Stefan—with the exception of a bushy mustache. With the couple was a plump, red-cheeked woman who had brown hair that escaped in little flyaway wisps from under her black straw hat. She waved at Frances and smiled.

The train gave a final jolt as it pulled to a stop. Frances managed to collect her carpetbag, hang on to Stefan, and climb down the steps to the wooden platform. Stefan, dropping his cardboard box, ran into his uncle's arms.

The plump woman made her way to Frances and held out a hand. "I'm Claudine Hunter, Miss Kelly. Thank you for escorting Stefan."

"It was my pleasure," Frances said. "He's a dear boy."

Miss Hunter's smile widened. "You'll be lodging with me in rooms at the Children's Aid Society. Perhaps you remember our offices on Amity Street. Andrew MacNair mentioned in his wire that you had been an orphan train child yourself."

"Yes, six years ago."

Stefan rushed over, tugging along his aunt and uncle, eager for Frances to meet them. The Gromeches spoke little English, but their joy at being reunited with Stefan was obvious.

Frances hugged Stefan and said goodbye. Mr. and Mrs. Gromeche had found employment at a hotel in New Jersey, and they were ready to take Stefan to his new home.

25

Miss Hunter led Frances to a buggy that was waiting for them. "It's a good thing the Gromeches arrived so soon after Stefan was sent out to be placed," Miss Hunter said. As the driver helped her climb into the back seat after Frances, she added, "If they had come a year or two from now, it might have been impossible to locate Stefan."

"Don't you keep records?" Frances asked.

"Such as we can," Miss Hunter answered. "We try to keep track of the children, but there are so many, so *very* many of them. Also, sometimes the foster parents move and don't tell us. Sometimes the placement doesn't work out, and instead of informing us, the foster parents will give the child to friends or relatives, and we'll lose contact. Sometimes there are deaths. Sometimes a child's name will be changed, even without official adoption. And the war, of course, caused great confusion." She shook her head and sighed. "This placing-out program is a very difficult task."

Not as difficult as it is for the children, Frances thought, remembering the strangers she had had to face at their stop in St. Joseph. She shivered with the same chill she had felt six years before when she had wondered if anyone would want the Kellys and prayed that those who did would be kind and loving. Frances and her brothers and sisters had always been close, and they'd clung together desperately after Ma had sent them west to new homes. It had been unbearably painful to be parted. And yet, she had to admit, Reverend Brace's placing-out program seemed to be the only way to keep so many children alive.

Miss Hunter had continued to chatter as though unaware of Frances's silence. She'd apparently changed the subject, because she cocked her head like a large robin and looked at Frances as though she'd just asked a question.

Frances blushed and said, "I'm sorry. I'm afraid I wasn't listening. I was thinking about my own orphan train ride."

"Of course, dear," Miss Hunter said. She patted Frances's arm. "Will you visit your former home while you're here?"

"Yes," Frances said. "And there are other places I remember that I'd like to see again."

"Good. You'll have this afternoon and most of tomorrow," Miss Hunter said, looking as pleased as if she'd arranged the timing herself.

It was early afternoon by the time Frances had stowed her carpetbag in one of the small bedrooms in the building.

"Perhaps you'll want to rest," Miss Hunter suggested, but Frances shook her head.

"I want to visit my old neighborhood," she said.

"And where is that?"

"West Sixteenth Street," Frances answered, remembering the row of crowded, soot-stained buildings, the constant smell of grease, boiled cabbage, and unwashed bodies.

Miss Hunter bit her lower lip and frowned. After a pause, she said, "Please be careful. There has been an epidemic of cholera in New York, and the authorities believe it festers in the slums."

Frances was offended. "Where our family lived was a poor area, no doubt about that," she said. "But *slums*? That's an ugly word. Are they now calling the neighborhood a slum?"

Even though she was embarrassed, Miss Hunter didn't give up. "Oh, dear Miss Kelly, what I'm trying to say is, it's not just the cholera I'm concerned about. Please, please arrange to return well before dark."

"I will," Frances said, and smiled. "Don't worry about me, Miss Hunter. I've long been able to take care of myself."

But Miss Hunter didn't smile back. "In the past few years your old neighborhood has been taken over by criminals. Things are different now."

4

FRANCES PAID LITTLE attention to Miss Hunter's fears. Hadn't there always been bullies and copper stealers on the streets near her home? And hadn't Mike taught her at an early age how to defend herself? She smiled as she left the Society's offices, walking past tidy rows of narrow brownstone houses with steep front steps. Some of them were decorated with pots of red salvia and pink geraniums, the blooms of summer.

She passed dry goods shops, which sold buttons and thread and bolts of cloth, greengrocers' with bins of shiny apples and hard, green pears, and small cubbyholes for dressmakers, confectioners, and barbers.

As she neared West Sixteenth Street, the shops became fewer as tenements crowded together. Here and there Frances saw open doorways and knew that the people who lived in the small, cramped rooms were trying to catch a bit of fresh air. Occasionally she saw someone sunning in a doorway. She smiled at an elderly man in a threadbare gray suit who chewed on an unlit pipe, and at a woman whose shawl had fallen back from her dark hair.

The man nodded, but the woman threw Frances a look of dark suspicion.

Frances was suddenly self-conscious about her own brown gabardine skirt; high-collared, white cotton blouse; high-buttoned shoes; and dark straw hat. Once she had dressed as this woman did, in homespun skirt and shawl, and—unless the weather was cold—her feet had been bare. Memories of her childhood came forth in a jarring jumble of sadness and joy. Frances took deep breaths and walked a little faster.

As her steps led her down West Sixteenth Street toward Ninth Avenue, Frances began to understand what Miss Hunter had been worried about. Small knots of children hung around doorsteps or jostled and pushed one another. They darted at some of the adults going past, snatched fist-size chunks of bread from the basket of a helpless old woman, and taunted a bent, arthritic man who walked with a cane. The man struck out in fear, connecting with the nose of one of his tormentors, who ran down the street bawling and bleeding.

Frances hurried to the aid of the elderly man, but he suddenly ducked into one of the tenements. She blinked in surprise as she stared at the poorly constructed building. The wood showed signs of being fairly new, but it was badly stained. Here and there were cracks in the siding that would surely let the cold winter winds blow through, and the windows

30

were small and grimy. This was the address at which she had lived, but the familiar tenement had disappeared, replaced by an even uglier, more ramshackle building. Frances clutched her reticule with trembling fingers. Where was her home? The people she had known?

A woman stretched out of a lower window and yelled to a group of children, "Go away! Get out of here! Bad boys, the lot of you!"

"Ma'am?" Frances called to her. "Pardon me, ma'am. Do you know what happened to the building that used to be here?"

"Bad fire. Burned to the ground." The woman sneered, and her words snapped with bitterness. "It didn't take the owner long to rebuild. Lost money, he did, until he built something else to cram people into."

Frances felt tears burn her eyes. The building had been cramped and dirty and unsafe, but the room in which the Kellys had lived was a warm and loving part of her life.

But now that room was gone. Her last tie to New York City was no longer here. "Oh, Da. Oh, Danny," she whispered. "How it hurt to lose you! Oh, how I miss you!"

Suddenly the woman in the window yelled loudly, "Tommy! Jimbo! Leave the lady alone or she'll be callin' the police on you!"

Frances felt a tug on her arm. She whirled, swinging her reticule to one side, out of the grasp of a short, dark-haired boy.

He fell against Frances, off balance, and she grabbed his wrist, holding it tightly.

"Let me go, miss!" he yelled. "I did nothin' wrong. I was just passin' by."

"What are you doin' in our part of town, anyway?" one of the other boys demanded of Frances. "Let Tommy go!"

Frances looked down into Tommy's dirt-smudged face. "Who is taking care of you, Tommy?" she asked.

"No one. I take care of myself, I do," he answered.

"You can get help," Frances said. As he struggled to escape, she held his arm and insisted, "Listen to me, Tommy! You don't have to live like this. The Children's Aid Society will send you west to a new home with foster parents to care for you. You'll have good food and go to school and—"

"Go to school?" Someone in the crowd laughed and shouted an obscenity.

Frances looked around, startled at the adults and children who had gathered.

"You and your kind stay out of here!" a man shouted.

"Leave us alone!" a woman yelled. "Think you're better than we are, do you? Come to take our children away?"

The woman in the window leaned so far out she almost fell. "Mind your own business, Sophie!" she screamed. "I seen what happened. Tommy tried to snatch the lady's bag."

"You begrudge the poor lad a few coins? Miss La-de-da's got many more where that come from!" Sophie yelled back.

"Poor lad, my eyes!" someone said, and laughed. "Best little thief, you mean. Mark my words, he'll be off to prison one of these days."

Soon bystanders were shouting at Frances, at Tommy, and at each other.

Suddenly the sharp shriek of police whistles split the air. Tommy looked up at Frances, and as their eyes met, she loosened her hold on his wrist. He slipped from her grasp and disappeared into the crowd.

A policeman elbowed his way through the crowd of people, many of whom took off in a hurry. He asked Frances, "Were you hurt, miss? Were you robbed?"

"No, Officer," Frances said. "Nothing happened to me. I'm all right."

"No thanks to Tommy O'Hara," the woman in the window called. "He tried to snatch her bag."

"He didn't succeed," Frances said.

"I know the boy. You have witnesses. You could bring charges," the officer said.

Frances thought of her brother Mike, who'd been tempted to become a copper stealer and had been caught. Without the help of Reverend Brace, who had asked the judge to let her brother go west for a second chance, Mike could have been sentenced to time in a prison called the Tombs. If she brought charges against Tommy, most likely he'd be sent to the Tombs. It was doubtful that anyone would come forward to give him another chance.

"I have no intention of bringing charges against the boy," she said.

The officer nodded and wrote something in his notebook. Then he raised his eyes to hers. "Beg pardon, miss, but you don't belong in this part of town. If you'll tell me where you're going, I'll see that you get there safely."

"I'm staying at the Children's Aid Society on Amity Street," Frances said.

"Then I'll walk you there," the officer told her.

Frances smiled at him. "Could you make it Fifth

Avenue instead?" she asked. "There are some places on Fifth that I want to see again."

"Again?"

"I once lived here," Frances said.

For an instant he looked puzzled. Then he returned her smile, apparently reassured by her mention of Fifth Avenue. "To Fifth Avenue it is. My pleasure," he said.

Frances and the officer chatted amiably. As they reached Fifth Avenue and Twenty-second Street, he said, "If you're going to be in New York a few days, maybe you'd like to attend the Policemen's benefit picnic supper on Saturday. I'd like to escort you."

Surprised but pleased, Frances smiled. "Thank you," she said, "but I must decline. I'll soon be going home to . . . to . . . Kansas." *I almost said 'to Johnny,'* she thought, as a rush of loneliness washed over her.

Frances parted with the officer. Just down the street, near Madison, she looked up at the square gray stone building in which she and Ma used to scrub floors at night.

It's not nearly as large as I remembered it, she thought with surprise. She pictured cranky Mrs. Watts and mean Mr. Lomax, who sent her on errands, threatening to dock her pay if she was even a minute late.

To her surprise, Mr. Lomax suddenly emerged from the building and strode toward her. Frances froze in place, momentarily terrified, just as she had been when she was a child. She'd received nothing from this thin, hawk-faced man but scoldings and recriminations.

But as Mr. Lomax looked up and saw Frances watching him, he tipped his hat and smiled.

34

"Good afternoon, Mr. Lomax," Frances said quietly. She relaxed, surprised that she no longer hated him. He was a pitiful thing, wrapped inside the shell of his own mean-spiritedness, and he no longer had power over her.

"G-Good afternoon, ma'am," Mr. Lomax stammered. She could feel his puzzled gaze on her back after he had passed her, and she giggled to herself, knowing that he'd wonder all day who she was and how she happened to know his name.

Frances walked up Madison to Twenty-third Street, where trees were thick and green and summer flowers bloomed in well-cared-for beds. Little girls in high-buttoned boots and tucked cotton dresses walked with their mothers or nursemaids in the late-afternoon sunlight, dodging the small boys in matching jackets and pants who darted and raced in games of chase and tag.

Even though it was almost time to return to the Society's building, Frances strolled over to where Fifth Avenue crossed Broadway. It was still an exciting vista of well-dressed women who visited the many shops with their window displays of ribbons, laces, and bolts of material for dresses to be made by skilled dressmakers. Every bit as showy as the window displays were a few wealthy women, wearing large, plumed hats. They rode up and down the avenue in their gleaming open carriages.

Frances remembered with a pang the beautiful doll she had once admired in the window of a nearby store. She crossed Fifth Avenue and stood before the shop's window once again.

The doll in the tucked and pleated pink silk dress was not there, of course, but another doll—equally lovable—was propped in the same spot. It was a baby doll, with a tiny white bonnet and lace-trimmed christening dress. Its arms were spread wide as though begging to be picked up.

"If only I had a little girl," Frances whispered as she clasped her hands together. "How I would love to bring her this doll."

But I don't, she told herself crisply. Besides, the doll would surely cost a fortune. She tore herself away from the window and headed toward the church her family had attended.

It was cool and silent inside, the heavy stone walls shutting out the noise from the street. Sunlight brightened the stained-glass windows, casting splotches of melting rose and blue and gold on the pews and altar. Votive lights flickered next to the tabernacle and in rows in front of the shrines at both sides.

Frances genuflected, then slipped into a pew and knelt on the hard wooden kneeler. How often, when she was a child, had she knelt with her family like this on the special occasions when they were able to go to Mass? Just as when she was young, she found comfort in the silence and beauty and love that seemed to swirl around her shoulders like a blanket.

She prayed for her family, and as she lit two votive candles she said the special prayer for the dead for Da and Danny. In her mind she could see their happy smiles, their loving faces, which had been so much alike. "I miss you," she whispered.

The lowering sun cast a final burst of color through the stained-glass windows, then dimmed. Frances hurried to leave, knowing she must return to Amity Street and the Children's Aid Society before dark.

5

As FRANCES WALKED through the front door, Miss Hunter rushed to greet her. She grasped Frances's arms in her eagerness. "Oh, Miss Kelly! We badly need your help!" she cried.

"Where? What has happened?" Frances pulled away from Miss Hunter and reached up to remove the long hatpin that anchored her hat.

"Oh, no, no. It's nothing immediate. That is . . . it's immediate, but . . ."

Frances waited patiently for Miss Hunter to collect her thoughts. Finally Miss Hunter said, "One of our agents—Mrs. Margaret Dolan—has become quite ill and is hospitalized."

"I'm sorry. What would you like me to do?" Frances asked.

Miss Hunter took a deep breath and let it out

quickly, her words tumbling with it. "Mrs. Dolan was to escort a group of children to Missouri. Now, of course, she can't, and there is no one else available to take the children, but it's been advertised in three towns when they'd arrive. I know that you're a teacher, and you know how to deal with children, so could you possibly take her place and escort the children on their journey?" Her voice faded to a squeak and she managed to add, "Please, Miss Kelly?"

"When are they scheduled to leave New York City?"

Miss Hunter clapped her hands to her face. "Tomorrow morning! I realize that if you take the job it will rob you of a sightseeing day in New York."

Frances suddenly realized that she had no further desire to sightsee in New York. Her happy memories were of another New York City at another time. She'd always have the memories, but it was time to come back to the present—and to the future, which lay in Kansas.

Miss Hunter took another breath, which brought pink back into her cheeks. "There are thirty children. We'll pack some food for them and give you money to buy them milk and bread and whatever else they'll need on the journey. The pay you'll receive for your trouble is not great, but it should meet your immediate needs." She didn't say "please" again, but her clasped hands and the begging look in her eyes spoke for her.

"I'll be glad to escort them," Frances said, then smiled as Miss Hunter sighed with relief. "The ride back, traveling alone, would have been lonely." She didn't speak her thoughts: *And it would have given me too much time to dwell on the argument I had with Johnny.*

"Thank you, thank you," Miss Hunter said as she fluttered around Frances. "A cup of tea, that's what you need. Oh! We're having an early supper. Well, there's still time for a cup of tea. And we'll arrange to have you meet the children and get acquainted, of course. Before supper. No, after supper."

Frances took Miss Hunter's hand and led her to a bench just inside the door—the very bench she had perched on, with Mike, Danny, Megan, Peg, and Pete, while they waited for a kind, soft-spoken woman named Mrs. Minton to ready them for their trip west.

"Sit with me for a minute," Frances said. "It will help if I know a little about the children before I meet them."

"Of course! But we'll need the list! I could never remember all their names without a list!" Miss Hunter sailed into the nearest office and back again, waving two sheets of paper as she plopped down on the bench next to Frances.

"Here's the railroad's schedule of stops—some for water and fuel, and some where you can buy fresh milk and bread. Most have privies, too. There will be privies on the train, as well. And here's the list of children. It's alphabetical," she said. "See—first are Emily Jean Averill, who is four, and her sister, Harriet Jane Averill, who is ten. Oh, how that dear girl worries about her little sister. She won't allow her out of her sight. Goodness knows what might happen if they're separated."

For a moment Frances and Miss Hunter stared at each other silently. The rush of pain that came from the memory of being separated from her brothers and sisters was almost too strong for Frances to bear.

She took a deep breath and said, "Please go on, Miss Hunter. Who are the other children?"

"There's the three Babcocks," Miss Hunter said. "George Henry is ten, Earl Stanley is nine, and their baby sister, Nelly Elizabeth, is three." She shook her head. "They're quiet children and keep to themselves. They're frightened and sorrowed for some reason. It's not the trip west, I'm sure. I've tried to learn more, but they won't open up to me. Maybe they will to you."

She glanced at the list again. "Nicola Boschetti. She's a lively child. Small for eleven, but happy and healthy. I just hope she'll find a home with a family who'll appreciate her hijinks and not wish they'd chosen a quiet, obedient daughter instead."

Miss Hunter sighed. "Now here's one I worry about. Belle Marie Dansing, nine years old. Belle was a foundling, left on a doorstep. She has no known parentage, and she was brought up in orphanages. There's prejudice against foundlings, and it's so unfair."

Frances felt a rush of tenderness toward this child. Had Belle ever felt a hug or known anyone's love?

Miss Hunter quickly read through the next few names: "Margaret di Capo, eight; Lottie Duncan, eleven; Walter Ray Emerich, five; and Philip Emery, four. They've recently come to the Society, and I don't know them well. It seems that Reverend Brace told me there was some kind of problem with Lottie, but I can't for the life of me remember what it was."

"A behavior problem?" Frances asked.

Miss Hunter's forehead puckered as she thought. Finally, she said, "I really can't recall. Isn't that dreadful of me to forget? Me oh my! With all these children and their names and backgrounds to try to remember, it's a wonder my mind doesn't give out entirely."

Frances smiled and patted Miss Hunter's hand.

"You're doing an excellent job. Don't worry. I've taught children with all kinds of problems. Lottie will be an interesting challenge."

Miss Hunter smiled. "Good. Well, I can almost promise you won't have problems with the next few children. Frank William Fischer, at twelve, is a fine young man, eager to go west. Daisy Ann Gordon is only nine and says she wants to be loved by parents more than anything in the world. Jack Greer is seven. His big brown eyes will melt your heart. Whoever gets Jack will be lucky."

Her eyes following her finger down the page, Miss Hunter said, "Now, here's Lucy Amanda Griggs, a ten-year-old waif from the streets. Landlord threw her out when her mother died. She's somewhat afraid of going west, but she's eager to have parents and a sister—a little sister. When I interviewed her, all she could talk about was having a little sister."

"I hope she gets her wish," Frances said.

"I hope all of them do," Miss Hunter said with a sigh, but she perked up at the next name. "Alexander Hanna. Eight years old and a real joy. And Virginia Hooper. She's ten." Miss Hunter smiled. "Virginia insists she's a princess and was switched with another child at birth."

"Does she remember her parents?" Frances asked. "How young was she when she was orphaned?"

"She was a foundling, left on the steps of a hospital. Her date of birth and her mother's first name were printed on a scrap of paper pinned to her blanket. She was taken in by a foster family in New Jersey, then returned four years later when the foster mother died. Virginia has lived in an asylum ever since."

"Dear little girl. She needed a family in her past, so she created one for herself," Frances said.

"She created a family, all right," Miss Hunter said, "and you'll never talk her out of it. She insists she remembers—names, places, everything."

Again her fingertip returned to the list, sliding to the next line. "David Paul Howard, eleven. Very quiet boy. Used to doing what others tell him to do. David lived off the streets until a slightly older friend brought him to us. He wanted David to have a real home, he said." She shook her head. "It's amazing how David survived this long.

"Here are some other recent arrivals: Mary Beth Lansdown, eleven; Jessie Kay Lester, nine; Edward Paul Marsh, eleven—ah, he's a caution; Marcus John Melo, twelve; Samuel Jacob Meyer, ten; Shane Howard Prescott, eleven; and Lizzie Ann Schultz, two. Lizzie is a darling. You can assign her to one of the older girls to care for on the trip. Most agents pair the little ones with the older girls. It's a great help with so many children to watch over."

"What about the children you just named? Any problems?" Frances asked.

"I can't promise you that there won't be problems. They're all old enough to get into trouble. Maybe some already have, maybe some are going to. I don't know. You'll just have to spot any potential trouble-makers and keep them in line."

Frances nodded. She'd found that a hug or even a friendly pat on the shoulder was often enough to reassure a child who just needed to know he or she was cared about. She wasn't worried about how the children would behave. She worried about how they would stand up to the terrifying ordeal of meeting strangers while wondering if they'd be chosen. She vividly remembered her own fears.

"Will Scott is twelve," Miss Hunter said. "He was brought to us by his father, who works with a traveling circus. Mr. Scott explained why he was unable to care for Will, but Will is in mourning for his father. He can't believe his father would send him away."

Frances gulped back the tightness in her throat. She knew what Will must be feeling.

"Then there's Adam John Stowe, eight, and Harry James Stowe, ten," Miss Hunter said. "That little one clings to his brother night and day. How they're going to be separated, I can't imagine."

She looked at the sheet of names and sighed. "The last two, now, may give you problems," she said. "Agatha Mae Vaughn, who's twelve, was banished from the orphanage she's lived in for years. She's a born troublemaker. Wait till you meet her. Her mind gets set on something and there's no budging her. I don't envy the people who take her in."

"Maybe, with a little love—" Frances began.

Mrs. Hunter shook her head. "You're very young, and love may seem to be the answer to everything, but with Aggie—" She smiled and said, "All I can say is, good luck."

Frances reached for the list. "That's all?"

"One more," Mrs. Hunter said. "Seven-year-old Caroline Jane Whittaker. Her father beat her, and she's very much afraid of him. He disappeared four months ago, soon after Caroline's mother died. The aunt who took Caroline in brought her to us because she couldn't afford to care for her. Caroline wants to go west to a new home, but she's frightened."

"Afraid she won't be chosen? Or afraid of finding the right family?" Frances asked.

"Oh, no," Miss Hunter said. "She's afraid that her father will come looking for her. She's afraid that he'll find her."

6

AFTER SUPPER FRANCES was introduced to the children. A plump, golden-haired little girl immediately raised her arms to Frances and said, "Mama."

"Aren't you a love," Frances said as she picked up the baby. "You must be Lizzie."

"Lizzie," the little girl repeated.

Miss Hunter beckoned to a thin girl with dark hair. "Mary Beth," she asked, "how would you like to be paired with Lizzie on the trip?"

Mary Beth smiled proudly and held out her arms. "She likes to have me hold her."

Lizzie cheerfully went to Mary Beth and giggled as Mary Beth nuzzled her neck, murmuring, "Don't you, Lizzie-Lizzie? Don't you?"

A tall, large-boned girl with a badly cropped fuzz

of red hair scowled at Miss Hunter. "You should have asked *me* to take care of her. I'm the oldest."

Miss Hunter's hands fluttered in distress. "I know you are, Aggie, but I thought—"

Frances interrupted, smiling at Aggie. "I'm sure you're very capable, Aggie. A three-year-old takes even more watching than a two-year-old. Suppose we assign Nelly Babcock to you?"

"No!" A boy, who firmly held his baby sister's hand, stepped forward. "I'm George, Nelly's brother. No one takes care of her but *me*!"

"And me!" A younger boy, with the same pale hair and red cheeks as Nelly and George, squeezed close to the pair.

This must be Earl Babcock, Frances thought.

"A little girl takes special care—" Frances began, but George interrupted.

"When she does, *you* can help me."

"Yes, I can," Frances said. She put an arm around Aggie's shoulders, surprised when the girl stiffened. "Aggie," she said, "I hereby make you my official first assistant. I'll need you to help me with all the little ones."

"She can't tell us what to do," someone said.

"Of course not," Frances said reassuringly. "She won't even try. She'll be helping me feed everyone during the day, make them comfortable at night, count noses at depot stops. . . . There's a great deal Aggie and I will have to together."

Frances could feel Aggie relax, but the look the girl gave her was wary, as though she didn't know whether to trust what she had heard.

"I was an orphan train rider," Frances told the children. "When I was Aggie's age I traveled to St.

Joseph, Missouri, with my brothers, Mike, Danny, and Pete, and my sisters, Megan and Peg."

George Babcock sucked in his breath and held his little sister so tightly that she squirmed to get free. His words were barely more than a whisper as he stared up at Frances and asked, "Did you stay together, miss? Were you all taken by the same family?"

Seeing the raw hope in George's eyes, Frances desperately searched for the right answer. "No, we weren't," she said. "But we all found good people to love us. And we loved them in return."

Her answer hadn't been enough, she realized. Despair replaced the hope in George's eyes, and he stepped back.

An insistent tug on Frances's skirt nearly pulled her off balance. She looked down to see Adam Stowe and smiled at him.

But Adam didn't smile back. His face was pale as he said, "My brother, Harry, and I *have* to stay together, miss. Our father said Harry was to take care of me. Doesn't anybody ever take *two* children?"

Frances squatted so that she could be at Adam's eye level. "Yes," she said. "Sometimes they do."

As Adam smiled, the color returned to his cheeks. Frances looked up at Harry, Adam's older brother. "You have to understand that many of the people who take in the children from the orphan trains can't afford to feed and clothe more than one child. Raising even one child is costly."

Harry nodded bleakly, but Adam said, "It's all right, Harry. She said *sometimes* people take two. We'll look for those people. We'll stick together."

Frances slowly got to her feet. Her chest ached with the hurt of what she and her brothers and sisters had gone through and what these frightened children

47

had in store for them. With all her heart she wished that Adam and Harry would be adopted together, and that the Babcocks wouldn't be separated, but she knew the chances of this wish's coming true would be very slim.

Frances went from child to child, getting acquainted. She could see fear in some of their eyes, a despairing acceptance in others. Three boys, however, had the jaunty, quick-witted good humor that had always been Mike's trademark, and she was drawn to them.

Small, wiry, redheaded Eddie Marsh—with a look of mischief on his face—grinned up at Frances. His arms rested on the shoulders of Marcus Melo and Samuel Meyer. "Me and my chums are all for this train ride to the West, miss," he said. "We heard those trains can go fast as a galloping horse."

"That they can," Frances agreed.

"Do the horses and trains ever race?" Marcus asked. "If I had a horse, I know I could beat any train, anywhere, anytime!"

"Quit your braggin'!" Eddie said, and elbowed his friend in the ribs. "You never rode a horse."

"Yeah," Sam echoed. "You ain't got a horse, and you're not likely to ever get one."

"Don't be so sure," Frances said. "Most of the people who take in the orphan train children live on farms, and there are always horses on farms."

The boys stopped jostling each other and stared at Frances. "Real live horses?" Marcus asked.

"Naw. Old dead horses," Eddie answered. He and Sam whooped with laughter.

Frances smiled at Marcus. "My wonderful foster parents drove me to their home in a wagon pulled by two fine horses. It wasn't long before I learned how to groom the horses and harness them."

"Did they let you ride them?" Eddie asked eagerly.

"Yes. Sometimes with a saddle, sometimes bareback, and sometimes I took them out hitched to a wagon."

"By yourself?" Sam asked.

"Oh, yes. All by myself."

For a moment she could almost see the thoughts churning inside the boys' heads. Then Eddie looked up and grinned again. "This goin' west . . . I'm thinkin' it won't be half bad," he said.

Excited, the boys ran off, and Frances turned to see a small, solemn-faced little girl looking up at her. Frances grasped for her name. Meg . . . Margaret. That's what she was called. Margaret di Capo.

Margaret crooked her finger at Frances, beckoning her to come closer. Frances squatted so that her face was level with Margaret's.

Although Frances smiled and waited patiently, Margaret didn't speak, so Frances finally said, "What is it, dear? What do you want?"

Tears spilled from Margaret's eyes, and her lower lip trembled. "I want . . . I want someone to love me," she cried, and flung her arms around Frances's neck.

Frances held Margaret until her sobs finally ended. "Someone will, little love. Someone will," Frances said.

She was determined that every single one of these children was going to end up in a happy home with loving people. Mr. Friedrich, the man who had been so cruel to Mike, came to Frances's mind. She quickly shook the memory away. At least she could make sure that these children would be happy as long as they were in her care.

As Frances settled Margaret into a chair with Jessie Lester, she saw that Margaret was clutching a tiny bundle of white. "What is that?" Frances asked.

"My rabbit," Margaret said. She opened her tightly curled fingers and held up a very small, white stuffed rabbit with embroidered black eyes and a pink nose. "His name is Flops. My grandmother made him for me."

Jessie looked solemn. "Her grandmother can't take care of her anymore. Her grandmother died."

As tears rose again to Margaret's eyes, Frances quickly said, "Margaret, why don't you tell Jessie about Flops? Can he do tricks? Do you ever make clothes for him out of scraps of cloth?"

Jessie spoke up again. "The butcher on our street kills rabbits for people to eat," she said.

Margaret burst into wails, and Frances picked her up and carried her to a sofa at the far end of the room. She held Margaret on her lap, stroking back her hair and crooning to her until the little girl settled down and dropped heavily into sleep, tears still on her cheeks.

A thin-faced girl of about ten came to Frances. Smiling, she held up a doll with a battered face. "This is Baby," she said. "I found her in a trash can, and now she's mine."

"She's lovely, Lucy," Frances said.

"Yes, she is, isn't she? That's because Mrs. Dolan washed and ironed her dress for me."

Frances watched Lucy as she walked off, showing her doll to Lottie. Suddenly Frances became aware that someone was standing beside her. She looked up to see Aggie Mae Vaughn. "Hello, Aggie," she said. "There's plenty of room here. Why don't you sit with me?"

Aggie slid onto the sofa and gave Margaret a critical look. "She's a crybaby," Aggie said.

"She's afraid," Frances told her. "I've cried when I was afraid. Haven't you?"

"No," Aggie answered. "I never cry." She hesitated a moment before she said, "And I'm never afraid."

Frances waited for what would come next. When she didn't speak, Aggie said, "Even when I broke a rule and had to go without supper, even when Miss Marchlander beat my hands with a ruler and told me no one would ever want to adopt me, I was never afraid, and I never cried."

"I'm sorry that someone hurt you," Frances said. She took one of Aggie's hands, sliding soothing fingers across her palm, but Aggie jerked her hand away.

"No need to feel sorry for me," Aggie said. "I learned my lesson. Miss Marchlander taught me not to let people hurt me. I'll never, never let anyone hurt me again. That's what I told her, and that's why she sent me away."

"Oh, Aggie," Frances began, and stretched out a hand again.

But Aggie stiffened. "She said I was a waif—somebody no one wants. But someone *will* want me. I'm going to have a real family. I'm going to live with people who love me and are good to me, until . . ."

Frances waited a moment, then asked, "Until what?"

Aggie shook her head, murmuring, "Never mind."

"You'll make someone a fine daughter," Frances

said, trying to smile reassuringly. Aggie looked as though she had something to tell her. Maybe she could be encouraged to confide her problem later.

In a small voice Aggie said, "I'm not a cute baby. And I'm not pretty like Mary Beth and Nicola. But someone will want me, won't they?"

"Of course they will," Frances said firmly, but she unhappily remembered some of the farm wives who only wanted foster daughters strong enough to handle the household chores. Aggie deserved a much better life than that.

Miss Hunter's voice carried throughout the room. "Bedtime, children. We'll arise early, because we'll have to travel to New Jersey to get the train."

There was a sudden hush, as if each child was afraid to breathe or even think. Frances knew what they were feeling. Tomorrow they'd begin a very different kind of life. Frances had been in their shoes. And Frances remembered.

"Come along now," Miss Hunter said. "Off to bed with you."

As the children filed out of the room, Miss Hunter spoke quietly to Frances. "You got along with them nicely. I knew you would, you being a teacher."

"I know how they feel," Frances said.

"These poor little foundlings and waifs? Well, as best you can, I suppose."

Frances didn't try to explain. She listened politely to Miss Hunter's advice about how to handle troublemakers, and how to arrange orderly visits to the small necessity in the railway car and to the privies at depot stops, and how to keep the boys from hanging out the train windows or climbing over the other passengers in the railway car.

But Frances's mind went from child to child. No

matter whether there'd been tears or smiles, each of them was facing a difficult journey.

"I'll be fine, and so will the children," Frances assured Miss Hunter. She meant what she said with all her heart and tried to push away the doubts that kept repeating, *Don't be so sure. You know as well as you know your own name, Frances Mary Kelly, that on this trip anything can happen.*

7

THE PLATFORM AROUND the depot was bustling with travelers and well-wishers; salesmen lugging heavy cases; a few nicely dressed children—two of whom stuck out their tongues at the orphan train riders, then hid behind their mother's skirts; gentlemen in stiff collars and tall hats; and uniformed policemen who roamed through the crowd, their eyes constantly searching faces. Here and there were a few ex-soldiers with shabby clothes, and a few beggars, who disappeared when they saw the policemen approaching.

Miss Hunter and a burly conductor helped Frances and the young orphan train riders squeeze through the crowd.

Caroline clung to Frances's skirts, burrowing into them as though trying to hide.

"Don't be frightened, Caroline," Frances said. She remembered that Caroline was afraid her father would come looking for her. "You're safe with me."

But Caroline continued to hide, warily peeping out to scan the faces of the people on the platform.

Frances checked her list. She read each name aloud, and made sure the child climbed the steps and got into the coach car—Caroline first, of course. It was a difficult task. Lizzie Schultz had been fussing too much for Mary Beth Lansdown to hold her, so Frances offered to carry the baby herself. Lizzie's plump little arms were wrapped tightly around Frances's neck, and she refused to let go.

Suddenly, to Frances's surprise, Lizzie was plucked from her arms. A deep voice said, "All the other children seem to be aboard. I'll help you with this one, ma'am."

Before Frances could react, a strong hand gripped her elbow. She was firmly and quickly escorted up the steps and into the coach car, where the children had already claimed their places.

Frances turned to the tall, handsome stranger who had helped her. He was probably not much older than she was. His chin and jawline were lighter than the rest of his sun-browned face, so Frances realized that until very recently he must have worn a beard. His eyes were a deep blue, and his curly hair was thick and dark. He was dressed in black and wore a flat, black, broad-brimmed hat pulled low over his forehead.

He removed his hat as he bowed and said, "Reverend Oscar Diller, ma'am." As he waited for Frances to answer, his eyes shifted to the children, then back to Frances.

Surprised that so young a man could be a

preacher, Frances smiled and politely answered, "Thank you for your help, Reverend Diller. I'm Miss Kelly, and I'm escorting these children to foster homes in Missouri for the Children's Aid Society."

"A highly commendable occupation, Miss Kelly," he answered. "If I may assist you in any way, please don't hesitate to request my services."

Frances wanted to laugh at his formality. Surely he was putting on airs. This couldn't be the way he always spoke. It didn't seem to fit. And there was a familiar, telltale softness in his speech that Frances had caught. "Are you bound for Missouri? Do you come from there?" she asked.

Reverend Diller answered, "I grew up in Missouri but came east to study."

With a parting nod he left Frances and sat with some of the children. Pulling down his hat brim to shade his forehead, he held little Philip up so that he could look out the window.

Frances was kept busy while the train was in the station. Some of the children wanted to change places. Some kept bouncing into the aisle. Harriet suddenly cried out and pointed to a man on the platform. "Look, Emily! There's Papa!"

Frances looked, too, and saw a man leaning against a support, his head in his hands as he wept.

"I told you Papa would come!" Harriet said.

Emily strugged to get free. "I want to see Papa," she insisted.

"No!" Harriet held her tightly. "Papa's crying. He doesn't want us to see him crying."

Tears ran down Emily's cheeks. "Why doesn't Papa come and get us?"

"Because he can't," Harriet said. "Remember? He told us that he loves us and wants to keep us, but he can't. He has no money to take care of us." Harriet burst into sobs. "He didn't want to give us away. Really, he didn't."

Frances fought back tears. Memories of when Ma had given them to Reverend Brace to send west tore into her heart in a burning pain.

"I know how much it hurts," she told Harriet and Emily. "When I was an orphan train rider, I had to leave my mother."

But they didn't even glance at Frances. Their gaze was riveted on their father, and they seemed to want nothing more than to look at him for what could be the last time.

A police officer entered the car and walked directly to Frances. "I was told these are orphans being taken to homes in Missouri. Is that right?"

"Yes," Frances said. "We're with the Children's Aid Society, the group organized by Reverend Charles Loring Brace."

The policeman touched the brim of his helmet. "Thank you, miss. Have a pleasant journey." His eyes quickly swept over the group of children as he moved to the back rows of seats, some of which had been filled by other passengers.

As he bent to question them, Frances realized that the policeman had completely ignored Reverend Diller. *Did the officer think the preacher is with us?* Frances wondered. She shrugged. *Well, what if he did? What difference does it make?*

Outside, the conductor shouted, "All aboard!" The police officer had already left through the connecting door at the back of the car, and Frances could see the cluster of policemen who had come together on the platform. None looked pleased, and Frances wondered what they were looking for.

The engineer gave a blast with a train whistle that frightened Nelly and Lizzie into shrieks. The lurch of the train into motion nearly threw Frances off her feet, but she regained her balance and hurried to soothe the little girls. She held Lizzie as the train began to move faster and faster.

"Hooray!" Eddie yelled. "We're off to the West!"

"And horses!" Sam shouted.

Amid the shouts and cheers from some of the children, Frances could hear Harriet's sobs. "Oh, Papa! When will we ever see you again?"

The rows of tightly packed houses disappeared, and the landscape changed to low, rolling hills. For a short while the passing scenery of small farms and animals kept the children's attention, but soon there were demands of "I'm hungry!" and "Please, miss, could I have a drink of water?"

"Aggie! I need you," Frances called, and Aggie stepped forward quickly, pouring water into tin cups for each of the thirsty ones.

"Thank you, Aggie," Frances said. "What would I do without you?"

Aggie didn't respond, but her chin lifted in pride. She looked down at Walter and Philip, who were jostling each other to be next, and fixed them in place with a frown. "Any more pushing, and you won't get water," she said. She handed the cup to a wide-eyed, obedient Walter and added, "And don't dribble!"

Although Aggie was being a little too stern, in Frances's opinion, she left Aggie without comment and went to soothe Margaret, who had burst into loud sobs. *Thirty children?* Frances asked herself. *It seems more like one hundred and thirty.*

Margaret grabbed Frances and held her tightly as she said through her tears, "Jessie told me there are

Indians in the West, and they're probably going to kill us."

"Well, there are," Jessie said. "Mrs. Spitz, down at the butcher shop, told us what the Indians do to the people they capture. She said . . ."

It was all Frances could do not to clap a hand over Jessie's mouth. There were people in every town who had to be the first to spread whatever terrible story they had heard, and unless Jessie was guided into another direction, she'd end up like Mrs. Garrett and Mrs. St. John.

"We'll have no more frightening talk like that, Jessie," she said. "It's true that our Union soldiers are fighting with some of the Indian tribes, but the battles are farther west. There are no battles where we will be going."

Margaret had stopped crying to listen. "Why are they fighting?" she asked.

"For the most part, they're fighting over who owns the land," Frances answered. "The Indians want to keep their land the way it was, so they want settlers and wagon trains and railroads to stay out. But there are many people in our government who feel we must expand our borders and settle the land coast to coast."

Margaret was curious. "Who's right?"

Frances thought a moment. "I don't know which side is right, and I don't know how to make right out of what could happen. I only know that every day many immigrants are coming into the United States. As they look for land on which they can farm and graze sheep and cattle, they move farther and farther west."

"Where they run into Indians!" Jessie added.

Frances took Jessie by the hand and led her to

59

another seat. "I'm going to let you sit with Nicola," Frances said, counting on Nicola's tough good nature to keep her from succumbing to any of Jessie's doomsday tales. "Belle, why don't you come with me? Margaret needs a seat partner."

She had no sooner resettled the girls when Reverend Diller joined her in the aisle. He smiled and said, "I overheard what you told the little girls. It's obvious that you're an intelligent woman. But you didn't give them the whole story about Manifest Destiny. Why not?"

Frances tried to ignore his smile. She had enough to handle without adding a political discussion. "Reverend Diller, Margaret and Jessie are two frightened little girls, only eight and nine years old. I was not about to explain the theory of Manifest Destiny. I simply told them what they needed to hear," she said.

"You need to tell them more about the expansion west. Otherwise they might think that the Indians have some kind of right to those lands."

Surprised, Frances looked directly into his eyes. "Perhaps they do," she said.

"Settlers are bound to move west and take over the land."

"I know," Frances said. "And they will. But can't it be done without bloodshed?"

Jack and Alexander, shouting and punching at each other, rolled into the aisle at Frances's feet, and she bent to separate them. When she finally cleared up the boys' misunderstanding, Reverend Diller had left and was slumped in a back seat, long legs stretched out before him, with his hat over his face, as though he was snoozing.

Frances smiled. She was intrigued by the reverend's strong opinions. If things hadn't been so hectic, she would have enjoyed having a long, uninterrupted political discussion with him.

The noise was rising, and Frances knew it was time the children settled down. The train would soon be stopping at a depot, and she needed to make sure there were orderly lines as they visited the privy. She decided to count noses.

With her list in hand, Frances checked on each child. Then she checked again. There weren't thirty children in the car. There were only twenty-nine.

"Sam! Marcus!" she called to the boys who had been sitting near Eddie. "Where is Eddie?"

"Don't know, miss," Sam said.

Marcus shrugged. "We haven't seen Eddie for a long time."

"Did he tell you where he was going?" Frances's heart began to thump faster. Surely Eddie wouldn't have jumped from the train.

"No, miss," Sam said, but he didn't meet her eyes.

Marcus squirmed and finally blurted out, "He said not to tell."

"You must tell me," Frances said. "I'm responsible for Eddie's welfare."

"Oh, you needn't fear, miss," Sam told her. "Eddie's always been one for takin' care of himself."

"Tell me," Frances said firmly. "Right now. Where is Eddie?"

Marcus gulped. "I wasn't lyin' when I told you I don't know. He just said to us, 'I'm off for a while, chums. I'm goin' explorin'.' "

"Exploring? On a train filled with strangers?"

Frances glanced in desperation at Reverend Diller's sleeping form. He had offered to help, hadn't he? He'd insisted that she call on him if she needed any kind of assistance. She couldn't desert the group

61

of children to go in search of one straying child, so—much as she hesitated to wake Reverend Diller—she decided there was nothing else she could do.

Frances bent over him, saying softly, "Reverend Diller. Please wake up, Reverend Diller."

He didn't move, so Frances touched his shoulder, lightly shaking it. "Reverend Diller—" she began.

Suddenly he let out a low, guttural cry, threw himself forward, and grasped Frances's wrist so hard that she yelped in pain. She was shocked at the dark terror and anger in his eyes.

"Sir! You're hurting me!" Frances said, and tried to pull away.

Breathing hard, as though waking from a nightmare, he let go so abruptly that Frances staggered back, off balance.

His face twisted in concern. "I—I'm sorry, Miss Kelly," he said. "I didn't mean to hurt you. I didn't realize . . ."

Frances rubbed the wrist that still felt the pain of his grip. "It's all right. I shouldn't have awakened you. I hoped you would . . . that is, you said . . ." She blurted out, "I need your help. One of my children is missing."

8

FRANCES PERCHED ON the edge of her seat, waiting and wondering. Would Reverend Diller be able to find Eddie? There was no doubt in Frances's mind that Eddie was used to taking care of himself. What if he was hiding somewhere on the train? What if he got off at the next stop and ran off on his own? How could she even hope to find him and bring him back? Frances keenly felt the heavy responsibility she had taken on. It was up to her to deliver these children safely.

Her wrist ached, and she absently rubbed it. She couldn't help wondering why Reverend Diller had awakened so frightened. Well, she had no time to worry about that now. Where was Eddie?

Finally, just as the train began to slow for the stop

at the depot, the reverend returned with Eddie in tow.

Frances hoped that Eddie had been firmly spoken to, but she doubted it because the boy was still jaunty and greeted her with a wide smile.

"I'm sorry, miss, that you was worried about me," he said. "I didn't think I'd be missed. I had to go explorin'. I like to see where I am and what's going on around me."

"I understand your curiosity, Eddie, but you must not leave the car," Frances told him.

"According to the conductors, Eddie explored the train from one end to the other," Reverend Diller said. Frances caught a twinkle of merriment in the reverend's eyes.

"And a mighty fine train it is, too," Eddie put in. "Oh, miss, can you believe it? There's a car that's got velvet curtains with gold fringe and thick paddin' on the seats that would make you think you were sittin' on somethin' as soft as a duck's bottom."

"A private car?" Reverend Diller asked.

"Yeah. Private. That's what they said before they threw me out," Eddie answered.

"Threw you out?" Frances was indignant.

"It's okay with me, miss," Eddie said cheerfully. "I had a right to go explorin', and they had a right to throw me out. It's nobody's loss. Give me half a chance, and I'd do it again."

"How many people were travelin' in this car?" Reverend Diller asked.

Eddie shrugged. "All I could see was a man and his wife—oh, and the feller workin' for them."

The train was slowing, and Frances had no more time to spend on idle chatter. "Thank you, Reverend Diller, for your help," she said, and led Eddie to join the other children, who were already bouncing in their seats, waiting for the train to come to a complete stop.

From the car's windows Frances could see the small wooden depot next to the tracks. She knew from her experience as an orphan train rider that the large water tank next to the depot would be used to replenish the train's water supply. Some of the firewood, in the huge pile near the water tank, would be transferred to the train. Only sparse, dusty clumps of grass grew in the yellowed dirt around the depot, and there were no passengers in sight, but a row of privies stood back by a small grove of trees.

"We'll form two lines to the privies," Frances told the children as the conductor opened the door. "Aggie will take the boys; I'll take the girls. We won't have much time before the train leaves, so no dawdling."

As she left the train, Frances saw Eddie glance at her right wrist, where her sleeve had fallen back.

"What happened to you, miss?" he asked, pointing toward the red marks on her skin. "How'd you hurt yourself?"

"It was an accident," Frances said, and pulled her cuff into place. "No harm was done."

Eddie ran to join the rest of the line, but Frances paused, placing the fingers of her left hand over the marks. Once again she wondered what had frightened Reverend Diller so.

There was no time to think more about it. Frances had to shepherd the children back onto the train, count them, and make sure no one had strayed into the small depot or the grove of trees beyond.

Finally each child was seated and the train made its jerking, swaying start. As it picked up speed, Frances opened her journal and began to write:

How greatly I am reminded of my own journey west. Riding an orphan train again, even though in a different capacity, makes me feel that I have come full circle. I think of the happy years I had with the Cummingses—a highly successful journey—and I hope that I can guide these little ones in my care into journeys that will be as happy as mine.

Eddie slid into the seat beside Frances, and she closed the journal.

"Sam and Marcus said I was in big trouble with you because of my goin' off to explore the train," he told her.

Frances smiled at him. "You're not in trouble with me, Eddie."

"You sure?"

"Of course I'm sure."

Eddie glanced up at Frances and grinned sheepishly. "Trouble and me—well, we sort of stick together, I guess."

"Maybe if you thought first—" Frances began.

Eddie interrupted. "I know, but I don't think first. Never have." He sighed again. "You've never been in trouble, or you'd know what I mean."

The train swayed around a curve, throwing Eddie and Frances off balance. As soon as they had righted themselves, Frances smiled and asked, "Where did you live in New York City?"

"Nowhere," Eddie said. "I mean, just anywhere I could sell a few newspapers, shine a few shoes, and earn enough to buy some food and stay alive."

"When I was your age I lived near Sixteenth Street and Ninth Avenue," Frances said. "Do you know that place?"

"Do I ever!" Eddie looked up at Frances in surprise.

"After my father died, I scrubbed office floors at night with my mother and sewed piecework during the day. My brothers Mike and Danny shined shoes."

"Like me," Eddie said.

"Like you. Only Mike turned to copper stealing and got caught. He wasn't a bad boy. He was a hungry boy and forgot the difference between right and wrong. He used the money to buy meat for our family's table."

Eddie's eyes were wide. "Did he go to prison?"

"No. He would have, but the judge let Reverend Brace send Mike west to a new home. He gave Mike a second chance to make a good life for himself."

Eddie leaned into the crook of Frances's arm. In a quiet voice he asked, "Did anybody want Mike? After what he done, I mean?"

Frances decided not to mention the terrible time Mike had with the Friedrichs. Eddie didn't need that. He needed reassurance. "An army captain and his wife eventually became Mike's foster parents," she said. "They're good to him, and he loves them very much."

Eddie thought a moment. "They didn't know Mike had been in trouble with the law?"

"They knew, but they still wanted Mike. In fact, it was Captain Taylor who told Mike that the West was a place for new beginnings and what counted most was what Mike would make of his future."

"His future? I never gave any thought to a future," Eddie said. "It seems to be enough trouble just tryin' to stay alive."

Frances hugged him. "You'll soon have a family who'll see to it that you have a good future."

Eddie turned to look up at Frances. "They won't hold what I did against me?"

"They won't even know about it."

She thought that would satisfy Eddie, but he said, "Sam told us that some lads aren't chosen, that they have to go back."

"That happens to only a very few. You'll be chosen," Frances promised. *Please*, she thought. *Please let my promises come true!*

Eddie grinned, and Frances smiled back. Eddie wasn't the kind to be down for long, no matter how bad things might look. "I'll change my ways," he said. "Matter of fact, I started changin' them back in New York City."

"Like going exploring?" Frances teased.

"I said I *started* changin' them. It's hard to do all that changin' at once."

"Captain Taylor said Mike was a fine young man, and you are too, Eddie. There'll be lots of good things in life for you," Frances said.

Aggie suddenly appeared at Frances's side. "Miss Kelly, some of the little children are getting hungry. Like Lizzie. Mary Beth said I didn't know what I was talking about, but I know when a baby gets fussy because she's hungry. I know a lot more than Mary Beth knows. And you did say I was sort of in charge. When are we going to feed the little ones?"

Frances pulled out her pocket watch and glanced at it. "It's not yet noon, but I think we're *all* getting hungry," she told Aggie. "I'll open the hamper, and if you'd like, since you're my special assistant, you can give everyone an apple—except Lizzie and Nelly, of course. I'll peel and chop their apples."

"We get apples?" Aggie's eyes lit in anticipation.

"Along with bread and cheese," Frances said.

She and Aggie set to work giving the food to the children. Some of the adults at the back of the car brought out food they'd brought with them, but Frances noticed that Reverend Diller had nothing to eat.

Frances motioned to him, and he came to the front of the car. "Please join us. We have plenty to share," she said.

He looked away in embarrassment. "I—I was in a hurry to leave. I didn't think about packin' food."

"Then please share with us," Frances said.

Daisy Gordon piped up. "Miss Kelly, David's already started to eat, and we didn't say a blessing."

Jessie nodded. "At the asylum we *always* said a blessing."

Frances turned to Reverend Diller. "Will you lead the children in a prayer, please?"

She folded her hands and prepared to pray, but he nodded toward Daisy and said, "I'd like to hear this little girl lead the prayer. She'd be happier with the prayer she's used to than the long blessin' that preachers say."

Daisy didn't need prompting. In a loud, singsong voice she recited, "Bless us, O Lord, for thy bounty which we are about to receive." She smiled, shouted "Amen," and bit with a crunch into her apple.

Reverend Diller took the food Frances had given him back to his seat, while Frances sat by the window, enjoying the bread and cheese and the scenery of softly rolling hills. But a cry from deep within her heart shattered this moment of peace. *Oh, Johnny— how much I miss you!*

9

It wasn't until long after nightfall that quiet settled on the railway car.

Frances had told all the stories and poems she could remember from her classroom readers to the thirty sleepy children. She'd helped make them comfortable on the hard coach seats. After the lantern had been extinguished and the railway car was lit only by the light of a full moon, she wandered among them singing some of the soft Irish songs that Ma had always sung to ease her children into sleep.

When most of the children had fallen asleep, some of them pillowing their heads on their seatmates' laps or shoulders, and no more lonely sniffles were to be heard, Frances removed her hat and relaxed in the front seat. She retrieved her carpetbag from under the seat and pulled out a pencil and the journal

Johnny had given her. There was enough moonlight so that she could see to write. She desperately wanted to put her thoughts about the children on paper to keep.

She stroked the blank page of the journal before she found herself writing about Johnny and how much she missed him. Had she been wrong to leave without talking it over with him? Had she hurt him too much to ever make things right between them? Frances sighed as she wondered if her questions even mattered. Johnny had turned away from her. He'd turned inward, obsessed with anger at those who had injured him. Johnny couldn't come to her with an open heart because his heart was filled with bitterness. She wrote:

> *When I return to Kansas, will I see Johnny ever again? What will my life be without him? Perhaps I should move to St. Joseph and live near Ma. Maybe it would be better to*

She jumped as Reverend Diller slid into the seat next to her. Flustered, Frances closed her journal with a snap.

"First off, I want to apologize for grabbin' your arm like I did," Reverend Diller said. "Sometimes I have bad dreams, and when you touched me I thought . . . Well, there was someone in my dream, and I was fightin' back. I didn't mean to hurt you."

"It's all right," Frances said. "It was my fault. I didn't mean to startle you."

Reverend Diller glanced at the blue book on Frances's lap. "What were you writing?" he asked.

"I keep a journal," Frances said. "I was about to write about some of the children."

"They're a handful. They've given you a hard day," he said.

Frances smiled. "No, they haven't," she said. "They're all very good children."

He slowly shook his head and smiled back. "One gives you a fright by runnin' off through the train. Others squabble or fight. The babies cry. They demand your attention the entire time. You call that *good*?"

"They're *children*, Reverend Diller. Why be surprised when they behave like children? If they all sat quietly, I'd be quite worried about them."

"I'd like you to call me Seth, instead of Reverend Diller," he said.

"Why, that may not seem a proper way to engage in conversation, but on this journey I expect it is acceptable. I've always felt there are, indeed, times to make exceptions, so I'll agree," said Frances. "But didn't you tell me your given name was Oscar?"

He cleared his throat and examined the tops of his shoes. Finally he said, "Seth is my middle name, but it's the name I've always gone by."

Frances smiled. "I'm sorry. I seem to keep embarrassing you. I shall call you Seth. My name is Frances Mary Kelly. You may call me Frances. How long have you been a preacher?"

"Not long," he said.

"Where did you study?"

"Study?"

"Yes. What school of divinity?"

He paused and smiled, as if in reflection. "Yale."

"It must have taken years of study, yet you seem so young."

Even in the dim moonlight she could see him blush. "I'm older than I look," he replied.

Before Frances could say another word, he asked, "How about you? Are you eighteen? Nineteen?"

"I'm nineteen," Frances answered.

"Most girls pretty as you would be married by nineteen," Seth said softly.

A rush of lonely feelings filled her heart, and Johnny's face came to her mind.

She didn't answer.

"I didn't mean to speak out of turn. I guess bein' a preacher and all makes me seem nosy," he said, and his smile was broad and friendly. Frances smiled back.

"Tell me about yourself," he said. "Where do you live? What do you do?"

At first Frances spoke haltingly. "I'm a teacher. I teach school in Kansas," she said, but as she saw the interest in Seth's eyes, she went on to tell him about her little house and the town of Maxville, built after the railroad came through.

Seth asked about her family, and when she spoke of traveling with her brothers and sisters on an orphan train, he reached over and squeezed her hand in sympathy.

Looking deeply into her eyes, he said, "I'm sorry you had such a hard childhood."

His dark, curly hair, his handsome face were so close to hers . . . Frances gulped and pulled her hand away. "It wasn't a bad childhood. There were many happy times, many good memories to think about."

"Are you tellin' me there weren't any bad times?" Seth asked.

"Of course there were," Frances answered, "but I try to keep those out of my mind. I'd rather think about all the good things that happened."

"That means you're hidin' from the bad memories."

"No, I'm not," Frances insisted. "I just believe that there's no reason to keep bringing up unhappy thoughts."

"There is for some people," he said. "Some of them need the anger and the hurt to help them remember."

Boldly Frances asked, "Are you talking about others you know, or are you talking about yourself?"

"Does it matter?"

"Yes, it matters."

Seth was quiet for a moment. Then he said, "I fought in the war. You couldn't understand what it was like."

"Then help me understand. Tell me what's making you unhappy." Maybe Seth could help her understand Johnny's bitterness.

"Have you ever seen a Union Army prison camp?" Seth asked. "No. Of course you haven't."

Frances gasped, but Seth didn't seem to notice. He continued: "Lice and rats and moldy food—what little there was to eat. Not enough blankets to go around in the winter months, not enough clean water to drink during the hot summer. And the hospitals . . . Prisoners who're brought there are in such bad shape they're expected to die." There was a long pause before he whispered, "I wouldn't die. I showed them all. I refused to give up."

"I'm sorry you had to go through such misery," Frances said, now understanding why he had awakened in such a frightened state, what horrible nightmares he must have. Did Johnny have nightmares like that? Seth had been in a Union prison and Johnny in a Confederate prison, but their complaints were the same. And their hatred of their captors was equally strong.

Frances sucked in her breath. What had she said to Johnny? The same held true for Seth. "Wouldn't you rather forget the unhappiness and get rid of the anger and the hurt?" she asked. "Can't you put the past aside and think about the future instead?"

"No matter. It's over now," Seth said. "I'm goin' home to Missouri."

"To your parents?" Frances asked.

"No. My parents died while I was away. I've made plans to join my older brothers."

A strange look came into his eyes, and he turned his head.

"Do they farm?"

Startled, Seth looked back at Frances. "Farm?"

"Your brothers. Are you going to be a visiting preacher, riding from town to town on Sundays and farming during the week? Is that what you plan to do after you join your brothers?"

He sat back. "Have you seen some of the Missouri farms that were burned out? Crops and livestock stolen? Everything gone?"

"The land can be reclaimed," Frances said. "Houses can be rebuilt."

Suddenly shedding his dark mood, Seth seemed to relax. "Let's talk about you. Are you goin' to be a teacher all your life? Or could it be you've got your heart set on bein' a farm wife, risin' before dawn to feed the chickens and hogs?"

Frances felt her face grow warm. "I—I haven't given my future much thought."

"Maybe you should," he said. "Maybe there's a far different future out there for you—a much more excitin' one."

"Seth," Frances said, "it's getting late. We both need our sleep."

Seth smiled. "Then sleep well. I'll see you in the mornin'." He rose and silently strode down the aisle.

Seth and Johnny, Frances thought. *The same bitterness, the same hatred of those who hurt them, the same inability to let go of the past and move forward. If there had been no war, what would Seth have been like? Would he have laughed easily? Planned for a joyful future? Hoped to be a good husband and father? Like Johnny? Like the Johnny I once knew?*

Frances tucked her journal away under the seat, then folded her jacket to use as a pillow. She rested her head against the jacket and closed her eyes. There was so much to think about . . . so much to do. . . .

A cry brought her to her feet, and she struggled down the aisle to where Lizzie and Mary Beth sat. The younger girl was upright, fists against her eyes, tears running down her cheeks.

"Mama!" Lizzie sobbed.

Frances scooped her up, murmured against the softness of her baby-fine curls, and carried her back to her seat. With her arms wrapped around the baby, who snuggled contentedly against her, Frances fell asleep.

She dreamed of Johnny. In her dream, he was on a train, traveling farther and farther away from her. She held out her arms and cried out to him to come back, but Seth stepped between them and Johnny didn't return.

10

A SMEAR OF PALE GRAY predawn light seeped into the car, waking Frances. She tucked Lizzie crosswise on the seat to finish her slumbers. Then she slipped into the small necessity at the end of the car to wash her face and brush her hair. As soon as it was coiled and anchored with combs on top of her head, Frances prepared to care for the children, some of whom were beginning to awaken.

Seth stepped to her side and smiled at her. "What can I do to help you?" he asked.

Pleased by his offer, Frances smiled in return. "According to the schedule I was given, we'll have a depot stop soon," she said. "There'll be a great deal to accomplish in a very short time."

He glanced at the hairbrush in her hand, and his

smile stretched into a grin. "Don't ask me to help with the hair bows and such. I'd be lost."

Frances laughed. "Then we'll find you another job."

He raised a finger to tuck a stray wisp of her hair into place, but Frances stepped away, her face growing warm. "You surprise me, Reverend Diller," she said. "You are being much too familiar with me."

"I apologize, Miss Kelly," he answered. "I don't mean any harm."

Aggie, her hair a tousled mop, sleepily staggered up the aisle, coming to a stop in front of Frances. She stared at Seth suspiciously. "I'm ready to help," Aggie said.

"You've just been given the day off," Seth told her. "I'll help Miss Kelly with the boys."

Aggie's chin stubbornly jutted out, and she stood as tall as she could. "The boys mind what I tell them," she said. "You're not one of us. They won't listen to you."

Seth stood his ground. "I offered my help, and Miss Kelly accepted," he told Aggie.

Quickly Frances stepped forward and began to brush Aggie's hair gently. "Goodness knows, there's a great deal to do, and I'm glad to get as much help as I can. I'd like Aggie to continue with her job of waking the boys and taking them to the privy when the train stops. She handles the younger children well. Reverend Diller, I'd appreciate it if you'd help me carry fresh milk from the depot to the train."

Tossing a smug look back at Seth, Aggie began waking the boys.

Frances quietly told Seth, "Being my assistant means a great deal to Aggie."

78

"I didn't think she'd care so much. She's a young girl."

"She's leaving an unhappy childhood in an orphan asylum and is traveling into a future that frightens her. She knows she may find someone to love her, or she may not. Anything that helps Aggie to feel a little bit special is important to her . . . and to me."

"Sorry," Seth said. "I only wanted to help you. I didn't think these things mattered to a child."

"You were once a child, Seth," Frances said as she started up the aisle. "Think about your own childhood and how you felt about what was happening to you. Try to remember."

The stop for wood and water was a short one. Frances, thankful that Seth had taken care of buying fresh milk, helped the last child aboard just as the engineer pulled two long blasts on the whistle.

All the children were wide awake now and hungry, so Frances lost no time in dividing the milk and thick slices of bread among them.

As soon as their stomachs were full, the car became a noisier, livelier place. Some of the children tried to lean from the windows for a better look at the countryside. Questions flew through the air along with the small flecks of soot that dotted clothes and faces.

"Look at that white house with two chimneys! It's so big. How many families do you think live in that house?" Lucy Griggs asked.

David Howard leaned forward and squinted. "Will we live in houses like that?"

"Naw. They're for swells," Eddie said. "But I don't see tenements. Where are the tenements?"

"Look!" Jack Greer shouted. "There's cows. Where do the cows sleep at night? Do *they* have a house?"

"Horses have names," Emily Averill said. "Do chickens have names?"

"When are we going to get to the people who'll choose us? How long will it take?" Aggie asked.

"We'll arrive at the first stop in eastern Missouri tomorrow. It's a town called Harwood," Frances said.

Suddenly, it seemed, the children remembered why they were on the train. The car fell quiet as everyone became absorbed in his or her own thoughts.

Lucy reached into the aisle and tugged at Frances's skirt. "Will you help me find a family?" she asked.

"Of course," Frances said. She slid into the seat beside Lucy and held her hand.

"I want a special family," Lucy said, "with a mother and a father and a little sister for me to love. I've always wanted to have a little sister."

"Lucy, dear," Frances began hesitantly, "if people already have a child, they may not come to find another."

Lucy's eyes shone. "Oh, yes, they will! You see, their little girl will want a big sister. She'll be looking for *me*." She held out Baby and said, "I'm going to share my doll with my little sister."

Frances hugged Lucy to her, unable to answer.

Ten-year-old Harry Stowe suddenly popped into the aisle next to her. Throwing quick glances back to where he'd been sitting with his brother, he lowered his voice and asked, "Can I talk to you?"

"Of course," Frances said. "I'm listening."

"Adam hangs on to me all the time. He's been doing that ever since Mama and Papa died."

Frances nodded as Harry went on. "If somebody takes Adam and somebody else takes me, I don't know what will happen to him." Tears flooded Harry's eyes as he added, "I don't know what will happen to *me*."

Frances put a hand on Harry's shoulder. "Harry, I'll do my best to keep the two of you together, but I can't make any promises."

Harry's shoulders sagged. "I'm scared, Miss Kelly. You don't know how scared."

"Yes, I do," Frances said. "I was scared, too, when I thought my brothers and sisters and I would be separated."

"I can't let anything bad happen to Adam," Harry insisted.

"We won't let anything bad happen to him," Frances said. "A few months after the placing-out, Andrew MacNair comes to each of the homes to make sure the children and the adults are happy."

Harry wiped a hand across his eyes. "But how can Adam be happy without me?" he asked.

Adam suddenly shouted, "Harry! Where are you?"

"Right here," Harry called. "Please, Miss Kelly. Please try to keep us together."

"I'll try," Frances promised, and fought to hold back her own tears.

She rose to continue down the aisle, but a sob stopped her. She looked down at David Howard, who was rubbing his eyes with his fists.

"Want to tell me about it, David?" Frances asked as she knelt next to his seat.

"I miss my chum, Mickey," David answered.

81

Frances patted David's shoulder. "Tell me about Mickey," she said.

David gave a long sniffle, squinted at Frances, and said, "Mickey's the best chum anybody could ever have. He's older than me, so he looked out for me. He's a street arab, and smart as—"

Frances interrupted. "What did you call him?"

David looked surprised. "A street arab," he said. "Mickey sold newspapers and shined shoes, and he took care of me. He said I'd never be anything more than a guttersnipe, and not a very good guttersnipe at that."

"Oh, David, I'm sure that Mickey didn't mean it," Frances told him.

David looked back at Frances with big eyes. "Yes, miss, he meant it," David said. "Guttersnipes aren't smart enough to be street arabs. I tried, but I couldn't take care of myself. So Mickey decided I should go west on an orphan train and find a family to take care of me."

"I—I'm sure Mickey was right," Frances said.

"Mickey's always right," David said matter-of-factly. "He said that a family would give me love and food and a good bed to sleep in, and even send me to school."

"That's true," Frances said.

"I'm not sure about school, though. I read some because Mickey taught me, but it's hard," David said.

Frances hugged David. "Mickey *is* a very special friend," she said.

David nodded as he whispered, "That's why I miss him so much."

Frances continued up the aisle to her seat. To her surprise, Seth was waiting for her.

"Hello, Mother Kelly," he teased. "Have you patted enough little heads and wiped away enough little tears?"

Frances sighed as she sat down beside him. "You haven't done what I asked you to do."

Seth was startled. "What did you ask me to do?"

"Remember your own childhood," she said. "No one can truly understand children unless he's able to remember how he himself felt as a child."

"Who's the preacher—you or me?" he asked with a smile. "You also told me to forget the past and look to the future."

"I told you to forget the unhappiness of the past, not the happy parts," Frances said.

Seth shook his head. "I can't—not yet," he said. "That's the fire that keeps me goin'." He paused for a moment, pulling out a battered silver pocket watch to check the time.

Frances noted the initials *SRC* engraved on its cover. *How odd*, she thought. *S could be for Seth, but that's his second name. And what could R and C stand for?* Maybe it hadn't always been Seth's watch. Maybe it had once belonged to someone else, like an uncle or grandfather. A relative whose last name wasn't Diller.

Suddenly Seth asked, "Are your parents still livin', Frances Mary?"

"My mother is," she said, "but my father died when I was a child."

"I lost both my parents in the war," Seth said. He leaned forward, balancing his forearms on his thighs, clasping his hands together so tightly his knuckles looked like white knobs. "That Union butcher, General Lyons, swept his troops across their land, stealin' their food and everythin' of value. Then the Federals burned the house and destroyed the crops. My parents tried to protest, and they were killed."

"Oh, Seth! I'm terribly sorry," Frances said.

"Sorry isn't enough," he grunted. "Nothin' can make up for what the Federals did."

While she struggled to think of the right words to comfort him, Seth blurted out, "The Federals only *think* they won. Wait until they see what revenge can do."

Frances gasped at the twisted bitterness in his eyes. "Revenge isn't the answer, Seth. It can't solve anything," she said. "As a preacher, you must know the only answer is forgiveness."

"I'm just one of many," Seth said quietly. "There are plenty of folks who are angered by injustice, and sometimes injustice demands revenge."

"Injustice *is* wrong," Frances said, "but there are much better ways to right wrongs than by getting revenge."

Seth didn't answer, and for a moment Frances was frightened. She was sure he had a plan already in mind. "What kind of revenge are you talking about?" she asked.

Seth didn't have a chance to answer. At that moment, shoving and yelling, Sam and Marcus tumbled into the aisle.

"Boys! Stop fighting!" Frances called, but they paid no attention. Seth had to separate them.

"Tell me what happened," Frances ordered, but they both began talking at once, and she couldn't understand them.

It seemed like forever before order was restored. By the time Frances had heard their stories—which

84

made little if any sense—the train was slowing for a scheduled depot stop.

Frances immediately began counting children. Finally she spotted Eddie, who lingered at the back of the car with Seth, and called to him to come forward and join the others.

"The train will make just a short stop," Frances said. "Remember to hurry."

"We hurry, hurry, hurry," Aggie muttered, "and then we get back on the train and sit and wait. What if all that hurrying and waiting doesn't do any good? What if when we get to Harwood, nobody's there to choose us?"

Aware of the shocked and frightened faces waiting for her answer, Frances said calmly, "You'll find a lot of good people in Harwood. They're as eager to meet you as you are to meet them." She put an arm around Aggie. This time, Aggie didn't stiffen. "Don't always expect the worst, love. Think about the many good things the world has to offer."

Aggie cocked her head as if thinking and said, "I don't know if you're right about good things being out there, Miss Kelly. So far, I haven't seen any."

By early afternoon the children were tired. Some of them dozed lightly and some slept soundly.

Frances leaned back, her bones aching from the hard wooden slats, and wearily closed her eyes.

"Pssst! Miss Kelly? Are you asleep?"

Frances opened her eyes just as Eddie slipped into the empty seat next to hers.

"I need to talk to you," he murmured.

"What is it?" Frances asked.

"It has to do with the preacher," Eddie said. "That is, if he *is* a preacher."

Startled, Frances whispered, "Eddie, what Reverend Diller does and says is his own business, not ours."

"Unless he's makin' it ours," Eddie answered.

"What do you mean by that?"

"I mean he spends a lot of time lookin' at you and thinkin' about you, and last night he went and cozied up to you after he thought we was all asleep."

"It's nothing like that," Frances insisted. "He just wanted to talk." But she found herself blushing.

"What I'm gettin' at," Eddie said, "is that some of what he told you last night don't add up. I'm no slouch at cipherin', so I—"

"Are you telling me that you listened to our conversation?"

Eddie raised wide, innocent eyes to hers. "I was on the seat just behind yours. I wasn't listenin' in on purpose." Before Frances could tell him that wasn't the seat he'd been assigned to, Eddie went on. "I don't know how long a preacher's got to study to be a preacher, but I'm guessin' it's years, isn't it?"

"Yes, but—"

"And he talked about bein' in the army—Confederate, if he was in a Union prison—and then in an army hospital. That didn't all happen overnight."

"I know," Frances said.

"I'm guessin' again—and I'm usually right—that he's not much more than nineteen or twenty."

"I agree," Frances said. "But I don't know why he'd lie to us."

"What he told you about bein' in the prison—that sounds real," Eddie said. "But he didn't talk about bein' a preacher, so I'm wonderin' if he is or ever was. I think he's just pretendin'."

Frances sighed. "Eddie, we have no right to discuss Reverend Diller behind his back. I'm sure he has a good reason for whatever he says or does."

After a pause, Eddie said, "There's somethin' else. At the last depot stop, Reverend Diller went into the office and sent a telegram."

"There's nothing wrong about sending a telegram," Frances said, but her mind was whirling. Her headache was worse. How she longed for a cup of hot peppermint tea!

"Should we try to find out what he's up to?" Eddie asked.

Frances spoke firmly. "No, Eddie," she said. "We must not pry into Reverend Diller's life."

Eddie looked at her sharply, and Frances realized that her words had sounded unconvincing—even to her. It was important to follow the advice she'd given Eddie—to stop and think before acting. "This is no time to try to make decisions," she said. "We're both tired. While we have a chance, let's get some sleep."

Eddie nodded agreement, seemingly content that Frances was keeping an open mind. He left her side as silently as he had come.

This is all nonsense, Frances told herself. *Seth's actions are none of my business.* She rubbed her temples with her fingertips, but try as she would she couldn't relax. She was afraid that something was terribly wrong.

She drifted into sleep, and when she awoke Seth was at her side, one elbow propped on the back of the seat so that he could face her.

"You were staring at me," she accused. "I felt it."

He grinned. "I admit it. You're mighty pretty to look at."

As Frances self-consciously tried to tuck stray strands of hair back into place, Seth said, "I wish we

87

could have some quiet time together, without all these children wantin' your attention."

"Seth," Frances said, "I was hired to care for these children. They have first claim on me."

"I'm glad no one else does," he said. "Have a claim on you, I mean."

Frances gulped. This conversation had gone far beyond playful teasing. "Seth, be serious," she said.

He smiled. "I am serious. You're an interestin' woman, Frances. You're sweet and kind, but I think you secretly love adventure and excitement."

"Really!" Frances began, but Seth continued.

"I mean it. Cookin' and washin' and cleanin'—that's not enough for you."

"Seth," Frances said firmly, "let's talk about something else."

"I'd rather talk about you," he said, "and about us gettin' to know each other better. After this trip is over and you're back home in Kansas . . ."

One of the children let out a wail, and Frances jumped to her feet.

"See what I mean?" Seth said. "There's so much I want to tell you. There's so much to talk about. I'm willin' to wait until this trip is over."

"But—" Frances said.

Seth interrupted. "Don't worry about my findin' you. That part will be easy. Wherever you go, Frances, I'll be able to find you."

11

THE NEXT MORNING, after their first stop, Eddie sidled up to Frances, who was helping little Nelly with a tangled tie on her bloomers. He thrust a folded section of newspaper at her and whispered, "Page four. Read it." He jerked his head in Seth's direction and added, "But not when the preacher's around."

As Frances stared at the newspaper while smoothing down Nelly's skirts, Eddie said, "I didn't steal it."

"I didn't think you had," Frances assured him. "You're a fine boy, Eddie, and you're too smart to steal."

Eddie looked surprised. "Nobody's ever called me a fine boy," he said. "You believe that, do you?"

"Yes, Eddie, I do," Frances told him.

"I like newspapers," Eddie said. "Especially newspapers from New York City. Reminds me of what I left behind. So when I saw this gentleman gettin' ready to board back at the last depot, and knew he was goin' to throw away a perfectly good copy of today's paper, I up and asked him for it. Then I read through it and . . ."

Eddie glanced at the back of the car again. "Better tuck that paper out of sight. The preacher will be here to talk to you soon. He sure spends a lot of time with you."

Wondering how much Eddie might have overheard the night before, Frances found herself uncomfortably trying to explain. "Reverend Diller needs someone to talk to—just as you do," she said.

"No matter. I just don't want him to see that news story."

Frances bent to tuck the folded newspaper inside her journal. As her fingers rested on the soft blue cover, she felt a pang of loneliness. Even though Johnny had rejected her, she didn't want to forget him. She couldn't forget him.

A shout came from one of the little boys. "Miss Kelly, I lost my dog!"

"That's Walter," Frances said. "His little stuffed dog never leaves his side." She stood and asked Eddie, "Why don't you tell me what the news story is about?"

Eddie shook his head. "Just read it."

But Frances had to tend to the children. She found Walter's dog on the seat under his jacket, but the requests and complaints and arguments didn't stop. The children were bored and restless. The closer they came to Harwood, the more nervous they grew and the more frequently they fussed and cried.

She had no sooner soothed Lucy, who had last-minute fears about not being chosen, than Will Scott began to sniffle. Frances squeezed into the seat next to him and handed him a clean handkerchief. He wiped his eyes and blew his nose, but Frances could see that he was embarrassed.

"It's all right to cry," Frances told him. "It's only natural. My brothers and sisters and I all cried when we came west on an orphan train."

"I'm not an orphan," Will said. "I have a father. Someday maybe he'll come for me."

Frances smiled and patted his shoulder. "We had a mother who sent us west to give us a chance for a better life than we'd had on the streets of New York. One day she did come."

Will looked up hopefully. "My father works for Carnaby's Circus. It's become a traveling circus, so maybe the circus will come to wherever I'm living, and Father will come looking for me. Do you think so?"

Frances skirted the answer and said, "I think your father misses you very much."

"He tried to teach me some of the circus jobs so I could work along with him, but I couldn't seem to learn to do them right. Mr. Carnaby wouldn't hire me." Will's voice dropped as he said, "I guess I can't do anything right."

"Of course you can," Frances said. "It takes special talents to work in a circus, but there are countless jobs that require entirely different talents. Life has many paths, and someday you'll discover the path that's right for you."

Will stuffed his damp handkerchief into the pocket of his jacket and sat up, his back straight. "You told us your mother came for you," he said to Frances, "so I'll keep looking for my father. Someday he'll come for me, too."

Frances didn't get a chance to read the newspaper until the children dozed. Remembering Eddie's caution not to let Seth see the newspaper, she checked on Seth's whereabouts. He was sleeping in his seat at the back of the car, his long legs stretched out under the seat ahead of his, his hat over his face. Frances pulled out both her journal and the newspaper, then opened the paper and began to read.

The major stories dealt with whites rioting in Memphis and the continued, sporadic fighting between Union and Confederate forces in Texas who wouldn't admit the war was over.

Then a short news item caught Frances's eye. It described the rise of robber gangs in the West, young men who had learned a new kind of warfare under Confederate raiders such as William Quantrill. The February robbery of the Clay County Savings Association in Liberty, Missouri, was called the first postwar bank robbery in the country.

Although none of the law enforcement professionals or witnesses quoted were absolutely sure, Frank and Jesse James were named as the suspected leaders of the band who stole cash, bonds, gold, and silver and shot a man to death.

The item went on to say that since the February robbery, banks had become a prime target. Suspects in other robberies were named: the Daltons; the Youngers, who rode with the James gang; and the Connally brothers.

Frances sighed. Riots, robberies, shootings, deaths . . . Lee might have surrendered the year before, but the hatred engendered by the war continued.

It wasn't until she was about to fold the paper and

put it away that she noticed a story near the bottom of the page: "Robbery at Gunpoint." Someone had made a small pencil mark in the margin next to the story. Eddie?

Frances scanned it quickly, reading about the robbery of the owner of a large and successful New York City dry goods store. Carefully, feeling the prickles that told her something was wrong, she read it again. The owner had given a description of the robber: long, dark, curly hair and blue eyes. The robber also had the same height, weight, coloring, and probable age as Seth. Frances well remembered that Seth, on boarding the train, had been newly shaved, the skin on his chin and jawline much lighter than on the rest of his face.

The robber's clothes had been different, too—Confederate jacket and cap. . . . "Police were hunting . . ."

Letting the newspaper fall into her lap, Frances stifled a moan. She thought about Eddie's suspicions that Seth wasn't really a preacher, that he was too young to have studied divinity and also served time in the Confederate army. These were concerns she should have examined but had put out of her mind because . . . With a shiver she tried to face the truth. Could it have been because she'd grown fond of Seth?

Frances didn't need to read the rest of the story. Apparently more than enough money had been stolen to enable Oscar Seth Diller—or whoever he was—to pay for a train ticket, a shave and haircut, and the preacher's clothing he was wearing.

As a traveling preacher he'd be above suspicion, Frances knew. It had been a lucky break for him that while the police had been searching the train depot for him a group of children from a religious institution had been traveling on the train and he'd been able to blend in with them.

Hurt and angry, Frances scowled. *How could a grown man hide behind children?* she wondered. *How could he use them—and me—to save himself?*

But her heart told her, *Be fair. You have no proof that Seth was the robber. He may actually be a preacher. He may be perfectly innocent.*

Do you really believe that he's innocent? she asked her heart accusingly. *Do you believe he's a preacher? Eddie read this news story and marked it. He tied it to the police officers who searched the train before we left. Eddie thinks Seth is the robber. And you do, too.*

Her heart said, *No. I don't want to think it. In a way he's much like Johnny. He's young and hurt and doesn't know what he's going to do with his life.*

Oh, yes, he does, her mind responded. *He's traveling to Missouri with a purpose. He's made his plans.*

What plans? I'm not sure he has any.

Find out what they are.

How? her heart asked.

Ask him, her mind told her.

But if I know, then I'll become a part of them. I'll have to do something about them.

What should I do? Frances asked herself at last. But there was no one with whom she could discuss the problem. The decision was hers alone.

She glanced at her pocket watch: one hour until they'd arrive in Harwood. Her heart gave a jump. One hour until the children would meet the people who had come to see them.

Jessie's solemn little face came to mind along with the unbidden thought, *If anyone comes.*

What was wrong with her? Frances wondered. *Of course they'll come. They must come. Please let them come!*

She put the journal and newspaper inside her carpetbag and pulled out a hairbrush and a handful of wide white ribbons.

As she prepared to begin tidying the girls and making them look as presentable as possible, Seth joined her. "There's not much time," he said.

"I know," Frances answered. "I keep thinking about how it was when I was an orphan train rider. I wish I could give the children extra courage to help them through the selection process. If only—"

"Don't talk about the children," Seth said. "Talk about us."

Frances was taken aback. "W-What?" she stammered.

"I wish you could come with me," Seth said.

"I—I can't. You know that."

"At least not for now, Frances Kelly." Seth smiled. "But, as I said, I know how to find you and that little schoolteacher's house of yours near Maxville, Kansas."

Frances put a hand on his arm. "Seth, please don't."

A yell rang through the railway car. Sam ran from Marcus, who tackled him at Frances's feet. Seth jerked the boys up and pulled them apart, but they continued to struggle.

"He called me a name!" Marcus shouted.

"He said I was a liar!" Sam yelled.

The struggles and complaints continued until Eddie wiggled through the knot of onlookers. "C'mon, chums," he said. "We're goin' to be in Harwood soon. You gotta settle down and get ready."

Instantly the fighting stopped. Both Sam and Marcus turned apologetic faces to Frances.

"Sorry we were scrappin'," Sam said.

"Yeah. We're sorry," Marcus added.

Frances studied Eddie. His eyes gleamed with a secret excitement as his gaze met hers, and he quickly looked away. The fight had stopped too suddenly to be real. Had Sam and Marcus staged a distracting fight to take attention away from Eddie? All she could hope was that Eddie would soon tell her what had happened and why.

Frances didn't have long to wait. She finished tying a hair bow that sat on top of Mary Beth's hair like a large white butterfly. "You look beautiful," Frances told Mary Beth.

"I wonder, did my mother ever tie ribbons in my hair?" Mary Beth asked. "I was so young when she died that I can't remember."

Lizzie, again in Mary Beth's arms, patted the bow in her own hair. "Pretty," she said.

"You *are* pretty," Mary Beth told her. "You're a very pretty baby. Someone will choose you right away." She glanced up at Frances. "I feel like Lizzie's my little sister. I'm going to miss her."

Frances beckoned to Aggie, who was watching beside them. "I've saved a special ribbon for you, Aggie."

Aggie took a step toward Frances, but stopped when Jessie said, "A ribbon won't do Aggie much good. Her hair looks like cat fur. How are you going to tie the ribbon so it will stay on her head?"

"I don't want a ribbon," Aggie said. "I don't need

one." She plopped into the nearest seat and stared out the window.

"Let's all sit down," Frances said, knowing that nothing she might say to Aggie right now would help soothe her feelings. "It's only half an hour to Harwood. We all look fresh and bright, and if we sit still, we'll stay that way."

Eddie was waiting for Frances as she took her seat.

Frances lowered her voice to just above a whisper. "You set up that fight, didn't you?"

Eddie nodded. "I'm sorry for all the yellin' and such, but the fight worked out fine. Seth Connally was kept so busy he didn't see me go through his carpetbag."

"Eddie! That's his private property. You didn't have the right to do that!" Frances stopped, suddenly struck by something else Eddie had said. "Are you talking about Reverend Diller? You called him Seth Connally."

"That's who he is—Seth Connally. Just like I thought, he's not a preacher and his name isn't Diller." Eddie didn't stop for breath. "He's got a big handgun in his carpetbag, along with a rolled-up Confederate jacket. And there were some letters from his brothers, and—"

"Eddie!"

"I didn't read 'em." He shrugged. "Mostly because there wasn't enough time. But I read a newspaper clipping that fell out of one of the envelopes. It told about the Harwood Central Bank and—"

Startled, Frances interrupted. "Why would—" She gasped as she remembered the newspaper story. "Connally! The Connally brothers! Seth said he was planning to join his brothers. To rob banks? To rob the Harwood Bank? We have to do something to stop him!"

"There's a telegraph—" Eddie began, but Seth squeezed into the seat with Frances and Eddie.

"No telegrams," he said in a low voice to Frances.

Eddie, who was squashed in the middle, tried to wriggle free, but he froze as Seth warned him, "The gun's no longer in my carpetbag. It's under my coat—where I can get to it fast—and I'll use it if I have to."

Eddie gulped and huddled against Frances.

"You aren't going to endanger these children, Seth," she said.

"The children won't be in danger," he said. He slowly shook his head. "I was going to tell you everythin' when we met in Kansas. I thought in the meantime I could trust you."

Indignantly Frances asked, "Trust me to do what? Stand by and allow you to get away with robbery? Don't you care about the children at all? You even used them to shield you when you came aboard the train."

He looked puzzled. "I didn't plan on them shieldin' me. It was just a matter of belongin' to your group. I wouldn't have done anythin' to hurt them." He stopped and tilted his head, looking at her questioningly. "How did you figure it out?"

"A newspaper story about the New York City robbery," she said. "And the fact that you may be dressed like a preacher, but you certainly don't act or talk like one."

Seth grinned. "Or think like one. As you reminded me, preachers don't hold with revenge, do they?" He reached out a hand and lightly touched her cheek. "Don't think badly of me, Frances. With a little for-

98

giveness on your part, we could be happy together. I'd be good to you, and you could be happy with me. You like me. You know you do."

Angrily Frances shook her head. "I did like you—as a friend—when I thought you were someone who could learn to put the war behind you. But I don't like what you're doing, Seth."

"I told you what happened to my parents, and what happened to me in a Union prison. I have a right to take revenge," he insisted.

"No, you don't," Frances told him. "You'll hurt innocent people."

"These so-called innocent people didn't care about what happened to me."

"Seth, they didn't have a chance. Anyhow, it doesn't matter. If you—"

"It matters to me."

"Seth, please—"

Seth reached across Eddie to grab Frances's arm, and she winced at the hard pressure of his fingers. "Listen to me!" he said in a voice that had suddenly become deadly serious. "We're runnin' out of time. I offered myself, and you turned me down. If that's the way you want it, then pay attention, because I'm goin' to tell you what to do. You haven't got a choice." He pulled out his watch and glanced at it. "Twenty minutes to Harwood. Right on schedule."

He pulled a kerchief from his pocket and tied it loosely around his neck. As he got to his feet he said, "Pick up my carpetbag, Eddie."

As Eddie gripped the handle with trembling fingers, Seth jerked him to his feet and held him by his collar. "Goodbye, Frances," Seth said. "Don't forget me. Someday I'll come find you to see if you've changed your mind."

Screeching, shaking, the train suddenly came to a stop. Some of the passengers cried out. A woman screamed, "Robbers! They're right outside our car!"

Frances turned to look and saw three men on horseback with a saddled horse in tow. The men wore kerchiefs like Seth's, but theirs were pulled over the lower halves of their faces, concealing them. One man rode to the front of the train. One kept his rifle trained on the car in which Frances and the children were riding.

Seth's voice softened as he said to Frances, "I'm sorry. I want to trust you, to know you'd stand by me no matter what, but I don't think I can, so I'm takin' the boy."

Eddie's face was white with fear. He struggled, but Seth yanked him backward, pulling him toward the outer door of the railway car.

"No! You can't take Eddie. I won't let you." Frances stood and faced Seth.

Seth drew out his handgun and pointed it at her. She heard a few whimpers of fear from the children and some gasps from the few adult passengers at the back of the car, but none of them dared to move or even speak.

"Didn't you hear me? I said you don't have a choice," Seth told her.

Frances stared into Seth's eyes as she slowly walked toward him and his gun. "You won't shoot me," she said, "and you won't hurt Eddie. There's a great deal of hatred bottled up within you, Seth, but there's still some goodness and decency. Let go of Eddie. Give him to me."

She saw the horsemen join forces again. Impatiently they rode toward the car Seth was in.

"Come on, brother!" one of them yelled. "We're wastin' time!"

Seth glanced quickly at the horsemen, then back at Frances.

"Give Eddie to me," she repeated.

Seth hesitated. Then, in one quick movement, he shoved the gun into his belt and pushed Eddie toward Frances. No longer a cocky street urchin, Eddie wrapped his arms tightly around Frances, clinging to her.

In two long strides, Seth reached the door of the railway car, shoved it open, and leaped down the steps. He ran to join his brothers.

As he jumped onto his horse and began riding away, Frances cried out, "Those men are going to rob the bank in Harwood! We have to stop them!"

12

WHILE THE TERRIFIED children clung to their seats, the other adults in the car jumped up. Some ran to peer through the windows, and a few got in the way of the conductor, who burst into the car to see if any of the passengers had been harmed.

"We're fine," Frances told him. "But what about the others on the train? Did the men rob anyone?"

"I'm afraid so," the conductor said. "Mr. Gladney's mad as a stuck pig. Mrs. Gladney's crying over losing her mother's pearl necklace."

Even though Eddie's smile was wobbly, he said, "She'll get her necklace back. The money, too."

"Son, it's not that easy," the conductor began, but Eddie turned to Frances. "Remember, I told you, the telegraph—"

"We're miles from town," she said. "There's no telegraph out here."

"But there are poles and wires right next to the track," Eddie said, "and next to the baggage car, in the mail car, there's telegraph equipment. I found it there when I went off on my own, lookin' over the whole train." As color came back into his face, his smile widened into a grin. "I'll go back there right now and tell the operator who the robbers are and what they're plannin' for Harwood. He can hook up his equipment to the telegraph line and wire ahead to the police—"

The conductor broke in. "Out here the law officials are the sheriff and his deputies."

Eddie tossed his head impatiently. "Whatever they're called, they'll be waitin' for those Connally brothers when they ride in."

Oh, Seth, what is going to happen to you? Frances wondered. Seth had made the wrong choice, turning his anger into revenge, but for a little while he had been a friend. He had had the potential to do good. If only he would realize he could change his ways for the better. Mike had. Seth could, too.

Johnny's face came to mind, and Frances's unhappiness grew. *Oh, Johnny, my dearest love,* she thought with determination, *it's too late for me to help Seth, but it's not too late to save you.*

Frances let Eddie go with the conductor to get the telegraph equipment. Before he left, she patted his shoulder. "I'm glad you're here, Eddie."

She attempted to calm the children, whose fear had blossomed into excitement as they discussed what had happened. "Seth Connally wasn't a preacher," she told them. "He pretended to be so the police wouldn't find and arrest him."

"What's going to happen to him, Miss Kelly?" Aggie asked.

103

"They'll shoot him," Jessie said matter-of-factly.

Frances shuddered. "Oh, no, Jessie. If Mr. Connally's caught he'll be arrested, along with his brothers. They'll be tried before a judge and jury. If they're found guilty, they'll probably be locked up in jail where they can't rob anyone else."

Frances tried not to think about Seth. If he was imprisoned again, his bitterness and hatred and desire for revenge were bound to grow. She would have helped him if she could have, but there was nothing she could do for him now.

Sam asked, "What if the sheriff doesn't catch the Connally brothers? Then what?"

"I don't know," Frances said, but she thought about Seth's words with dread. "I'll come and find you," he had told her. He could do that easily. He knew where she lived. A shiver ran up her backbone.

The train gave a sudden jolt, throwing people into their seats. Frances grabbed the back of one seat, managing to keep her balance. "Sit down, children," she said. "We'll soon be in Harwood."

During the remainder of the ride Frances thought about the calm and friendly support of Andrew MacNair and Katherine Banks as they helped the Kellys and the other children over their fears. *I must be like them*, she thought. *The children need me.*

A muffled whimper came from across the aisle. *At least I can try*, she told herself. She hurried to pick up four-year-old Philip and held him close. As she hummed a lullaby, he stopped sniffling and relaxed against her. *What a dear little boy you are*, Frances thought. *Someone will be lucky to get you.*

As the train began to slow on its approach into Harwood, Frances stood and faced the children. Some looked back at her with fear in their eyes. A few faces were pale and pinched with worry. George Babcock tried to hold tightly to Earl and Nelly, who clung to him in desperation. Adam Stowe, tears rolling unchecked down his unhappy face, grasped his brother Harry in a stranglehold. Only Eddie, who had returned from helping the conductor, Sam, and Marcus kept up a smiling, poking, shoving, teasing manner; but as Frances looked into their eyes, she saw three scared boys hiding behind their brave masks.

Frances smiled. "You're going to discover many fine people who want very much to meet you," she said. "Some of you will find new families among them."

Jessie spoke barely above a whisper. "What happens if we don't?"

"Then you'll still have me," Frances answered. "I'll be right there with you. I won't leave you until you all find homes in which you'll be happy."

"You promise? You'll stay with us?" Lucy Griggs asked.

"I promise," Frances said. "Part of my job is to make sure that you all have good homes."

"How many stops are there?" Mary Beth asked.

"Three," Frances told her.

"And then what?" Marcus asked. "At the Society they said you brought a lad back because no one wanted him."

"That's not true," Frances said. "I brought Stefan back to New York City because his aunt and uncle came to the United States and asked for him soon after his orphan train left for Kansas."

"He had family," Daisy said in wonder. "A real family."

"I have a mother," Frances told Daisy. "I love her

very much, and she loves me. But I also have a foster mother and father, who took me in when I was thirteen and raised me as though I were a child of their own. A family doesn't have to be a mother and father and a child to whom they've given birth."

"Then what is a family?" Daisy asked.

Frances thought a moment before she answered. "A family is a circle of love," she said.

"Love?" Lucy echoed.

Frances smiled. "That's right. Love given and love returned."

Lucy smiled and hugged her doll. "Did you hear that, Baby? Love is a circle," she said.

As the train came to a stop, Frances could see a swarm of people outside, most of them staring at the train as though they were trying to see through the windows. A tall, broad-shouldered man strode toward the train, heading for their car.

The conductor opened the door and ran down the steps with his stool, but the tall man stopped him. Bounding up the steps, he entered the car, swept off his wide-brimmed hat, and spoke to Frances.

"Ma'am," he said, "I'm Sheriff Malloy. I take it you are Miss Frances Kelly and you have a boy here in your care named Eddie Marsh?"

"Yes," Frances answered. As Eddie stood trembling, clutching the back of the seat ahead of him for support, Frances automatically stood protectively between him and the sheriff.

"Eddie hasn't done anything he shouldn't," Frances said firmly. "I can vouch for him."

The sheriff smiled. "I didn't mean to rile you. I shoulda said right off that I came to thank Eddie for the information he gave the telegraph operator. That was smart of you, Eddie. We got our robbers—three of them, that is—afore they hit the bank, and we got the Gladneys' money and jewelry back."

Solemnly he shook Eddie's hand.

"Hip, hip, hooray for Eddie!" Sam shouted, but only a few of the children joined him. Most of them stared at the sheriff or at the people on the train platform who excitedly peered through the windows at them.

Frances cheered for Eddie, but as soon as she had the chance she asked the sheriff, "Which of the Connally brothers got away?"

"The one who rode the train," the sheriff said. He quickly added, "But don't worry. We've got men out lookin' for him. We'll soon round him up."

"Poor Seth," Frances murmured to herself. She knew Seth was deeply troubled. Would he ever get the chance to redeem himself?

"Are you all right, ma'am?" Sheriff Malloy asked. "You look kinda pale. It's hot here, even for July. Is the heat botherin' you?"

Frances took a deep breath, willing Seth out of her mind. "I'm all right," she said. "But I would like to ask a favor of you. Will you escort us, please, as we march to the Methodist church?"

"I'll be happy to, ma'am," the sheriff said.

Frances turned to the children. "Pick up your luggage, boys and girls. We'll leave this train and walk two blocks to the place where we'll meet the people who have come to see you. Come on, now. Remember . . . you're wonderful children, and I'm very, very proud of you. The families who'll get you will be lucky, so hold your heads high and smile."

As Frances climbed down the steps of the car she felt a strong pull at one side of her skirt. Caroline pressed so closely that Frances nearly stumbled.

107

Reaching down to stroke Caroline's hair, Frances said, "You're safe with me, love. Don't be afraid."

Caroline raised her head and surveyed the platform. "I looked and looked, but I don't see him," she whispered.

Frances knew that Caroline meant her father. "Take my hand," she said, and pulled Caroline to a position at her side. "We're going to meet the people who have come to find children to love."

The sheriff easily cleared a path through the bystanders on the platform, but two women spoke loudly, and Frances could hear their remarks.

"Look at them little waifs."

"I heard that some of them was left on doorsteps. Never had a proper father."

"And some are picked up right off the streets of New York City!"

"Um-hum. And passed off as being proper as you and me, but we both know that living on the streets the way they did, they've got to be little criminals."

"Maybe not all of them. Look at that little girl. Don't she look sweet and pretty?"

"That little boy, too. Cute as a bug. But that big girl, now. You can't say she'd take a beauty prize."

A gentleman in a high collar asked the man next to him, "Which one of the children was the boy who saved the bank?"

"It's gotta be that one who's smiling and waving at us. He's not shy at taking his bows. He heard you ask about him, I reckon."

"Did the bank manager give the boy a reward?"

"Reward? Why should the boy get a reward? He's only a child."

There was a great deal Frances would have liked to say to these busybodies, but she held her tongue and marched briskly past them down a dusty street to the Methodist church.

She led the children past the seventy or eighty people who crowded the room, to a raised platform on which three rows of stools had been arranged. A stout middle-aged woman stepped up next to Frances and pointed to three people seated in chairs at the side of the room. "I'm Mrs. Judson, and that's my committee," she said. "We know most of the people around these parts, which is why the Society asked us to serve. If you have any questions about anyone who wants to take in a child, you just ask us."

"Thank you," Frances said.

She seated the smaller children in front, the larger in back. When the children were ready, the sheriff raised his voice, so that it boomed against the back wall. "Quiet down," he bellowed. "Listen to what Miss Kelly has to say."

Frances looked at the many faces, and for a moment she was thirteen again, studying the crowd, looking for expressions of kindness and laugh lines and smiles, hoping that she and her brothers and sisters would find happy homes. Her heart beat faster, and she had to will herself to calm down.

She cleared her throat and began, as she'd been told to do, by explaining a little about the Children's Aid Society and what it hoped to accomplish with the placing-out program. She went over the rules about treating each child like one of the family and making sure he or she was schooled and taken to church through the age of fourteen—just in case the onlookers hadn't paid attention to the advertisements that had been sent out.

Then she introduced each child in turn, giving only names and ages.

Finally she invited the people to visit the stage and become acquainted with the children. "I hope there will be many of you here who will come to me and arrange to take a child," she said.

A buzz like that from a busy beehive filled the room as husbands and wives looked over the children and discussed them with each other. A young woman, her hat askew, ran to the stage and held out her arms to Lizzie.

"Mama?" Lizzie asked, and went right into the woman's arms.

"Oh, you precious child! You have to be ours!" the woman said as she hugged Lizzie.

"If you'd like to make arrangements to take her—" Frances began, but the woman didn't let her finish the sentence.

"We would! Oh, we would! Look at those beautiful eyes. She's so much like our own little girl would have been." She lowered her voice and said, "We lost our baby last year." The woman refused to let go of Lizzie for even a moment, even to let her husband hold her.

Another woman stepped up behind her. "I'm Mrs. Howard Smith," she said. "My husband and I also came to get a little girl. The two-year-old may be spoken for, but what about that pretty child you called Nelly? She's a darling. I tried to get her to come to me, but her brother won't let go of her."

"His name is George," Frances said. "And Nelly's other brother is Earl. They're hoping that someone will want to adopt the three of them together."

The woman gasped. "Three? It's not likely anyone could afford to take *three* children."

"They don't want to be separated," Frances said.

"It's up to you to make the decision, isn't it, and

not them?" the woman asked. "My husband and I raised five boys. Now we'd love to have a little girl. We'd be good to her and school her, and take her to church on Sundays, just like you said."

"Let me have a minute to talk to the children," Frances said, but before she walked over to George, she stopped to speak to the committee members, who sat in chairs at the side of the room.

"What do you know about Mr. and Mrs. Howard Smith?" she asked.

A bald man pursed his lips and nodded. "Good people," he said. "Raised a passel of boys, none of whom went bad. One son read the law and set up his practice down in St. Louis. Another's working at the store with Howard."

"They want Nelly Babcock," Frances explained. "If they take Nelly, it will separate her from her two brothers. They all hoped to stay together."

One of the committee members rolled her eyes. "Wouldn't children ask for the moon, if they thought they could get it!"

Mrs. Judson smiled sympathetically at Frances. "We went through this last year. It's a hard job to find homes for large groups of children. I'm always saddened when we have to put some of them on the next train." She glanced at Mrs. Smith, who stood where Frances had left her. "I've known Rose Smith for years. She's a good woman, and she's always wanted a little girl."

Frances sighed and said, "Thank you. I'll take your advice." With an aching heart she explained to George and Earl, "I can't take the chance on finding people who'd be able to adopt three children. I was told that the Smiths would be very good to Nelly and give her a happy home."

Earl's face was drained of color. "Will we be able to visit Nelly? Can we see her often?"

"I don't know," Frances said. Tears were streaming down George's cheeks. Nelly patted George's face and looked puzzled.

"Why you crying?" Nelly asked.

George's defenses broke down completely, and he began to sob.

Frances wrapped her arms around all three children. She knew how much sorrow they were feeling. But she also knew that this could be Nelly's only chance to find a loving family. "I'll give you the Smiths' address so that you can write to Nelly," she told the boys.

Giving them time to say goodbye to their little sister and steeling herself to their heartbroken tears, Frances reluctantly took Nelly from George and carried her to Mrs. Smith.

Mrs. Smith's smile lit the room. "Oh, darling Nelly, you're going to be mine!" she cried, but Nelly, realizing what was happening, stretched out her arms to her brothers and began to wail at the top of her lungs.

Frances, forcing back her own tears, handed out papers to a number of eager foster parents, but occasionally there was an eruption of tears on the stage, and she hurried to try to solve the problems.

"Nobody picked me!" Margaret sobbed. She clutched her rabbit tightly.

"They've just begun meeting the children," Frances told her. She pulled out a handkerchief and wiped Margaret's eyes. "Smile," Frances said. "You're such a dear girl, when people see that happy smile, someone is bound to want you."

Frances paused. At the back of the stage Eddie was entertaining a group of fascinated listeners by acting out the exploits on the train. "So there stood the robber, with his gun pointed straight at me," Eddie said. He raised and pointed an imaginary handgun at a woman, who gave a little jump and squealed. "But he wasn't going to get the best of me—not Eddie Marsh, who knew his way around the streets of New York City from the time he learned to walk."

Chuckling at Eddie's performance, Frances walked on.

Although many of the children were surrounded by smiling or curious adults, Aggie sat miserably alone on her stool at one side of the stage. With an aching heart Frances saw Aggie glance hopefully at two of the couples who came near, but none of them approached her.

Frances started toward Aggie, but a middle-aged couple unwittingly stepped in front of her. They stopped next to Aggie and examined her as though she were a bolt of cloth.

"She's a strapping big girl," the woman said to her husband. "She's not much to look at, and that red hair's a sight, but I'm sure she can handle plenty of hard work."

The woman suddenly took Aggie's upper arm in her roughened hands and squeezed the muscle.

Her face mottled red with anger, Aggie jerked her arm away. "Don't touch me!" she shouted at the woman.

"Well, I never!" the woman exclaimed. "Hard worker or not, I don't want a rude child like you!"

As the woman and her husband stomped off the stage, Frances put an arm around Aggie's shoulders. "Pay no attention to people like that," she said.

"I don't want to go with them," Aggie insisted.

"You don't have to," Frances told her.

"I—I don't want to be kitchen help. I want somebody to love me."

"Somebody will."

Aggie seemed to shrink inside herself. "Maybe Mrs. Marchlander was right. Maybe no one can love me."

"Aggie, dear, forget Mrs. Marchlander. She was wrong," Frances said. "Forget these people who were rude to you. I wouldn't have let you go with them in any case. You weren't sent here to be an unpaid worker. You were sent to be part of a loving family. Look for the family who'll choose you. If you see people coming to talk to you, smile at them. I know you must have a beautiful smile."

"Smile just so they'll choose me? That's like begging. I can't do that! I can't!"

"Then smile because *you'd* choose *them*. Can you try?"

Aggie lifted a woebegone face to Frances. "I guess I can try," she said.

Frances was needed to help a young couple fill out papers for Philip, so she left Aggie, hoping for the best.

Caroline Jane went willingly with a pleasant young man and woman. She tugged at Frances's skirt and whispered, "They'll take care of me, and my father won't be able to find me, will he?"

Frances knelt and put her arms around the little girl. "You'll have a new life with people who'll love you. Try to forget the unhappiness of your old life. Will you?"

Caroline nodded agreement, but tears rolled down her cheeks. Frances kissed her goodbye, tears blurring her own eyes. Were Caroline's fears real? Would

114

her father try to find her? Frances hoped and prayed that only the best would come to this frightened child.

Margaret bounced up and down as she said good-bye to Frances. "Someone did want me after all!" she exclaimed. She clung to the hand of her new foster mother, smiling as though all her wishes had been answered.

Frances said one goodbye after another, each time hoping that the right decision had been made and both the child and the foster parents would be happy. *But how can we really know what lies ahead for these children?* she asked herself. *All we can do is hope for the best.*

Finally the room had cleared of the people who had come either to take a child or to gawk. Frances asked Mrs. Judson to go through the papers so that Frances could make sure the information was complete and accurate. Seventeen of the thirty children had been chosen. "Thanks be that Emily Jean and Harriet Averill are going to the same family," Frances said to Mrs. Judson.

Mrs. Judson ran her finger down the list she'd drawn up. "Nelly Babcock and Lizzie Schultz—the babies and toddlers are always chosen first. Philip Emery, he's just four and cute as a button. He was bound to be a first choice. Next we've got Frank Fischer, David Howard, Will Scott, Marcus Melo, and Sam Meyer, which is no surprise. Farmers need boys who can help with the heavy chores."

Frances felt a stab of concern. How well she remembered Mike's terrible treatment at the hands of Mr. Friedrich! She said, "Mrs. Judson, you vouched for the people who chose the boys. You said you knew them. They'll be good to the boys, won't they? Surely they didn't come here just to get free farm labor?"

Mrs. Judson looked solemnly at Frances. "Have you ever lived on a farm?"

"Yes," Frances answered.

"Then you know the hard work that's involved. Rise before dawn and work until after dark. Every member of the family pitches in." She relaxed, patting Frances's hand. "The people who chose the boys are all good people. They won't abuse the boys. They'll treat them like their own children."

Frances nodded.

"By the way, Will won't live on a farm," Mrs. Judson said. "The couple who picked him—Sara and Otto Wallace—raised eight boys, all of them grown or off to school, and they're lonely. Otto is a well-respected doctor in a nearby town. Will may eat plenty of chicken, because sometimes the only way people can pay their doctor bills is with chickens or eggs, but he'll have a happy life."

Mrs. Judson went on with her list. "Caroline Jane Whittaker, Margaret di Capo, Mary Beth Lansdown, Nicola Boschetti, Lottie Duncan, Alexander Hanna, Virginia Hooper—" She stopped and smiled. "That Virginia's a caution. I heard her tell her foster parents that she's really a princess who was switched with another child at birth. Well, knowing the Johnsons and how much they wanted a little girl, they'll undoubtedly treat her like a princess."

Frances thanked Mrs. Judson and her committee members, then gathered the children who were left.

Eddie sidled up to Frances, a worried look in his eyes. "I was a hero back at the train," he said, "but I guess no one was lookin' for a hero. I heard two people say they wanted a quieter, more well-behaved child, not a lad of the streets like me."

Frances smoothed back Eddie's hair from his forehead. Such a tough boy, but with such open, vulnerable eyes. Eddie reminded her so much of Mike when he was young. "We've got two more stops," she said. "You'll have a family soon."

But Eddie's confidence was ebbing, she could tell. "The lads back home would have been proud of me," he said.

"And rightly so. *I'm* proud of you, too," Frances told him.

Mrs. Judson stepped up to Frances and waved a list. "Here's where the remaining children will be put up for the night. These are all good people who'll feed them supper and breakfast and have them at the station tomorrow morning in plenty of time to catch the train."

"Thank you," Frances said.

"As for you and the boy here," Mrs. Judson added, lowering her voice, "Sheriff Malloy and his wife are putting you up at their house."

"That's very kind," Frances said.

Mrs. Judson's eyes widened. "Oh, it's not to be kind," she said. "That robber who was on the train with you—"

"Seth Connally," Frances prompted.

"Yes, Seth Connally. As I was saying, he'll figure it out, if he hasn't already, that the two of you probably had something to do with setting the sheriff after him and his brothers. Since there's nothing to say that this Connally won't come back, the sheriff thinks you'll be a lot safer under his own roof."

13

SARAH MALLOY, WHO was as soft and plumply rounded as a feather bed, smiled and hugged Frances as they were introduced. "It's a wonderful thing you're doing, helping to find parents for orphans and waifs," she said.

"I'm glad I was able to rely on the committee," Frances answered. "I'd never have been able to figure out, among all those people, which would be good parents and which wouldn't."

Sarah's eyebrows rose and wiggled, as though she knew secrets no one else could know. "Hummph!" she sniffed. "I'm afraid the committee can be counted on just so far."

"What do you mean?" Frances asked.

"Think about it. Is Zeke Colley, who owns a feed store, going to tell you not to give a child to a good customer, even though he knows the man is after a free farm worker and nothing more? Or will Effie Jerome snitch on her best friend, even though she knows her friend has a temper that can't be matched and has been known to take a heavy switch to unruly children?"

Frances pressed a hand against a painful knot that had suddenly appeared in her chest. "If I've made some mistakes, maybe it's not too late to correct them. If you'll give me names—"

Sheriff Malloy tossed his hat at the top of a coat rack that stood just inside the front door of the small, cozy living room. "Now, Sarah, don't go stirrin' up Miss Kelly about somethin' that didn't happen. I was there. I saw who got the children, and they were all good, law-abidin' folk."

"Whatever you say," Sarah said pleasantly. She busily straightened a lacy antimacassar that sprawled over the back of a nearby upholstered chair, as if she wanted to show she didn't really agree with her husband. "Miss Kelly—" She beckoned toward a short hallway. "Put your hat and baggage in the first bedroom. You'll share it with our girls. Eddie can sleep on a pallet in front of the fireplace in the living room. Then join me in the kitchen. I'm making fried chicken and mashed potatoes for supper, and you can lend me a hand if you wouldn't mind."

"Not at all, you are very kind, Mrs. Malloy."

"You may call me Sarah, dear."

"Then please call me Frances," she replied.

Frances made sure that Eddie was comfortable before she went to help Sarah with supper.

"Will Seth Connally come back, like they think?" Eddie asked.

"No, he won't," Frances answered. "He's too

smart to try a senseless act like that." She ruffled his hair as she added, "All you've got to worry about is how much of Mrs. Malloy's chicken and mashed potatoes you'll be able to eat."

Eddie relaxed enough to smile, so Frances left him and walked into the kitchen.

She had questions for Sarah, but she didn't have to ask them. Sarah wanted to know about every child chosen, and she had comments to make about each set of foster parents. Frances was prepared to learn the worst, but with relief she soon found that Sarah's remarks were no more damaging than the tittle-tattle that went on at church suppers:

"Oh, she makes out to be the frugal one, but it's a fact that she sews fancy lace on her bloomers."

"She won first prize with her apple pie, but it wasn't her receipt at all. It was her sister's."

"A well-dressed feller came 'round, claimin' to be his brother, and didn't he have his nose in the air, but it turned out they weren't brothers at all but second cousins, and the cousin had walked out on a wife and six children."

Sarah glanced sidelong at Frances. "That robber that John thinks might come back—how did you get to know him?"

"He was a passenger in our car on the train," Frances answered.

Sarah rolled her eyes. "You took up with a strange man on the train?"

Frances ignored the shock in Sarah's voice. "No. I didn't take up with anyone. Half a dozen adults sat in the seats at the rear of our car. Mr. . . . uh . . . Connally was one of them."

"But he must have talked to you. He must have

told you what he planned to do." Sarah was so intent on hearing what Frances had to say that the chicken pieces sputtering and sizzling in the pan began to burn.

Frances wrapped a towel around her hand and slid the large, heavy iron skillet to one side of the stove. Sarah, embarrassed, jumped to turn the pieces so that they would brown evenly.

Knowing that Sarah would keep after her until she answered her questions, Frances said, "He told us just before he left the train. He was going to take Eddie hostage. I stopped him."

"My land!" Sarah exclaimed. "Weren't you afraid?"

"Yes, I was."

"And aren't you afraid now that he might come back?"

Frances thought a moment. Seth was intelligent, and there had been much he'd learned as a soldier— when to hide and when to pick the right time to make his move. He wouldn't return to Harwood for her. It would be too dangerous for him. If he came for her, it probably would be after she'd arrived back home . . . alone. Yes, she decided. That would be the time and the place. Frances knew this just as certainly as if she had received a mental message from Seth. Cold chills ran up her backbone, and she shivered.

"There, there, I knew you were afraid," Sarah said with satisfaction, "but you don't have to worry. Where else could you be safer than in the sheriff's own home?"

Soon the Malloys' two daughters were called inside to supper. The older, about fourteen, Frances guessed, had washed at the pump by the back door;

but it was obvious that the younger, who must have been no more than seven, had settled for some hasty splashes at her face, leaving streaks of dirt.

"We've got company," Sarah said. She moistened one end of a towel and scrubbed hard at her squirming daughter's face.

As she helped carry platters of food to the sturdy table that filled one corner of the living room, Frances saw with surprise that she and Eddie weren't the only guests for supper.

A brawny man with a gray beard slowly unwound his long legs and raised himself from a low upholstered chair to greet her.

"I'd like you to meet Sheriff Duncan, from over in Clay County, Miss Kelly," Sheriff Malloy said. "I've been fillin' him in on Seth Connally, in case he shows up in western Missouri."

Sheriff Duncan's voice rumbled deep within his throat. "Pleased to meet you, Miss Kelly. We'll do our best to catch Connally. Don't you worry none."

"Thank you," Frances murmured. She fumbled with the chair where Sarah directed her to sit, hoping that she wouldn't be asked about Seth. What could she tell them? That he was a bitter, unforgiving man bent on revenge? No. There was more than that. There was still goodness within Seth. He had proved it when he had done as she'd asked and hadn't taken Eddie.

Sheriff Malloy sniffed appreciatively at the steaming platter of fried chicken, bowed his head, and said a very quick grace.

Plates were passed to be filled, and Frances was gratified to see that Eddie began eating without hesitation. He appeared to be bouncing back from the hurt of not being chosen at this first stop. He'd be in good spirits tomorrow, she was sure.

During dinner the two men dominated the conversation. Between mouthfuls, Sheriff Duncan began talking about the robbery of the Clay County Savings Association back in February.

"It was one of the first bank robberies for Frank and Jesse James and their gang," Sheriff Malloy added.

"Now, wait. There's some doubt the James gang were the ones who done it," Sheriff Duncan told him. "We've got witnesses that swore Frank was in Kentucky at the time and Jesse was home sick in bed."

"Nobody on the scene recognized the James brothers?"

"Oh, sure. We got witnesses who'll swear the boys were there. We just have to figger who's tellin' the truth and who isn't."

Eddie, obviously fascinated by what the men were saying, looked back and forth from one to the other. Frances sighed. This was not the kind of conversation an impressionable young boy should be hearing.

Sheriff Malloy chuckled. "Maybe you should get Wild Bill Hickok into it. You heard what just happened over in Springfield, didn't you?"

"About him shootin' somebody named Tutt who won Bill's watch fair and square in a poker game?"

"Yeah. The way I heard it, the next day he stood at the corner of the public square, right smack in the middle of the city, and waited two hours for Tutt to come by. Called him out and shot him in the heart."

Eddie gasped, and his mouth dropped open.

"When's Bill going to be up for trial?"

"I don't know, but chances are he'll be acquitted. Tutt could have been lucky and got off the first shot." Frances put down her fork. "He killed a man over a watch?" she asked indignantly.

"There was an argument somewhere in there, too," Sheriff Duncan said.

"No matter," Frances said. "He killed a man. He should go to prison."

"We're talking about Wild Bill Hickok, ma'am," Sheriff Duncan said in surprise. "He's pretty well known for helping to bring law and order all the way into Kansas. Surely you've heard of him."

"Yes, I have, but it doesn't matter how well known he is," Frances said. "A murderer should go to jail."

Sheriff Duncan spoke slowly, as though he were trying to explain something difficult to understand. "But it wasn't murder, ma'am. It was a call-out. Either man could have shot first. Bill did. Tutt didn't. It was as simple as that."

Eddie nodded solemnly, along with the men.

"Kill or be killed?" Frances asked. "That's not what life is all about."

Sheriff Malloy broke in by speaking to his friend. "Women don't understand these things," he said. "I think Sarah's even given up tryin'. So there's no use explainin'."

Frances glanced at Sarah. "I'm very tired," she said. "May I please be excused? Eddie, too?"

"I'm not tired," Eddie said. He edged his chair a little closer to Sheriff Duncan's.

"Yes, you are," Frances told him. "And we have to rise early tomorrow to get under way."

Sarah said, "Make yourself comfortable in the girls' room. The girls will share the bottom half of the

124

trundle bed. You take the top. I'll make a pallet for Eddie near the fireplace."

"But I'm not sleepy," Eddie complained.

"Good," Sarah said. "Then you can help the girls wash the dishes."

Satisfied that Eddie wouldn't be subjected to an evening filled with stories about outlaws, Frances left the room. After she removed her tightly laced corset, she happily rubbed her back and sighed with relief. She changed into a nightdress and robe and washed her face and arms. It was the first time she'd been able to change her clothing since she'd left New York City.

Before she crawled into bed under one of Sarah's neatly pieced quilts, Frances opened her journal. In the light from an oil lamp she wrote about what had happened on the train, and she wrote about the children who had been chosen. Then she wrote about what she had been longing to write about but had pushed aside—her love for Johnny.

Johnny and Seth—they're so much alike in spite of being Union and Confederate in their feelings. If they had met on a battlefield, they would have tried to kill each other. If I tried to point out similarities, they'd hotly deny they had anything in common. Yet both are wrapped up in cocoons of resentment and hatred. Nothing else seems important to them. Seth's goal is revenge, and I pray that Johnny doesn't take the same path.

Johnny refused me, so in turn I refused him. Was I right to do so? I don't want to lose him. I can't.

Isn't love stronger than hatred? I just hope that somehow I'll have the chance to prove this is true.

125

* * *

At midmorning, after a hearty breakfast, Frances and Eddie returned to the depot, accompanied by Sheriff Malloy.

He plopped down on the platform a heavy basket of fresh biscuits, cheese, and apple cake that Sarah had packed for the children and surveyed the area around the depot. "Sarah doesn't understand I can't be a packhorse *and* a watchdog, too," he said. "You don't see Connally around, do you?"

"No," Frances answered.

The sheriff kept his eyes on the window in the small building and added, "I'll just have a quick look-around."

Many of the children had already arrived. Frances greeted them eagerly, then thanked the kind people who had given them shelter for the night.

Soon all the names on her list had been checked except one—that of five-year-old Walter Emerich.

"I can't leave without Walter," Frances told Sheriff Malloy. "Is there someone we could send after him?"

The sheriff smiled and pointed up the road. "There's Jake and Effie Kleinhurst coming now, and they've got a little boy with them. Is that Walter?"

"Yes," Frances said. "Thank goodness!"

As Jake Kleinhurst stopped the wagon, his wife jumped out, not waiting to be helped. She picked up her skirts and ran through the dust toward Frances. She was a small, thin woman, and she shyly ducked her head as she said, "I'd thought about asking for one of the children, but I wasn't sure if we should or not. I didn't know how it would turn out. What if the child wasn't happy? Or what if Jake and me weren't happy?"

In the distance a train whistle blew, and the children clustered more tightly around Frances. Jake, with Walter in tow, hurried to join his wife. "Come out with it, Effie," Jake said.

Effie Kleinhurst raised her voice and spoke rapidly. "Please, miss. Walter is the child Jake and I have dreamed of having. Please . . . it's not too late, is it? May we take Walter to raise?"

Frances smiled at Walter. "Is this what you'd like, Walter?"

"Yes," Walter said, and he raised his arms to Jake. "Pick me up, Papa," he said.

"I'll vouch for the Kleinhursts," Sheriff Malloy told Frances. "They've got a good-size farm, and they'll make the boy happy."

Jake's face reddened with pleasure. "I'm gonna get Walter a pony," he said.

Frances rummaged through her carpetbag, found the right papers, and, with the Kleinhursts' help, filled them out just as the train chugged into the depot.

She hugged Walter goodbye and helped the other children up the steps into one of the cars. "It's a short trip," she told them. "We'll be in Springbrook soon after lunch."

While the children settled into their seats, Frances quickly glanced around the car. *Don't be ridiculous*, she told herself as she realized she'd been looking for Seth.

Sheriff Malloy put the heavy basket next to the rack for baggage and shook Frances's hand. "You be careful, now, y'hear?" he said.

"I will," Frances told him.

"I'm willin' to bet you haven't seen the last of that young man."

Frances didn't answer, but she secretly agreed. Last night she'd been sure that Seth would wait until she'd arrived home—that is, if he decided to put in an appearance—but now she wasn't so positive. Seth was impulsive, and he would be angry. It was possible that he'd intercept her en route.

"The conductor's goin' to watch out for you, and I telegraphed the sheriff's department near Springbrook to keep an eye on you and the boy while you're there," Sheriff Malloy assured her.

"Thank you," Frances said, trying to keep her voice from trembling. "But I don't think we'll have any trouble."

"Maybe not," Sheriff Malloy said, "but it's best to keep an eye out for it and head it off before it gets started."

Irrationally, Frances wanted to laugh after he left the railway car. The sheriff sounded as if he were reporting an approaching storm. *In his own way, Seth is a storm*, she realized, and for the first time she wondered what she'd say or do if he suddenly appeared.

14

THE TWELVE CHILDREN making the second lap of the journey were quiet and almost too well-behaved. Frances knew they were worried about having to go through the selection process a second time, and she wished it were in her power to ensure that every one of them would find a happy home. She told them stories she invented on the spot; she sang to them; and she made up riddles. She played a form of "I Spy with My Little Eye" with the farm animals and objects they could see from the windows, but those who joined in did so halfheartedly. It was obvious that their minds were on the coming ordeal.

At one point Frances felt that she was being watched, and she glanced up quickly. Near the back of the car, on the aisle, a pair of eyes looked back at her from under a flat, broad-brimmed black hat.

The man sat slumped down in his seat, his legs stretched out under the seat in front of him. A tattered Confederate jacket lay across his chest as a blanket, and its collar hid the lower part of his face.

Seth? Frances looked away. For a moment she felt faint, and her hands trembled.

"Miss Kelly, I'm hungry," Daisy complained.

Her voice broke the spell, and Frances pulled herself back to the job at hand.

Frances opened the basket and let Aggie pass the food to the children. Frances's mind raced. *I'll ignore him. The man couldn't be Seth . . . or could he? If he is Seth, why is he here? What does he want? Maybe—if he is Seth—I can convince him to give himself up.*

Frances gave a small groan. She couldn't bear not knowing. *There's only one thing to do, and that's confront him*, she thought.

She straightened and took two steps down the aisle before she saw that the man had left. She walked to the empty seat, looking for Seth's familiar carpetbag, but there was no sign that anyone had ever been there.

"Pardon me, sir," she said to the gentleman in the high collar and tightly buttoned suit jacket who sat by the window. "Can you tell me, please, the name of the gentleman who was sharing this seat with you?"

The man looked surprised, then shrugged. "Didn't pay him much attention," he said. "He got on the train the same stop you did. That's all I know."

Puzzled, Frances returned to the children. It wasn't likely the man had jumped off the moving train. He'd probably just moved to another car. And he most likely wasn't Seth at all but just another ex-soldier making his way home.

130

Every few minutes one of the children would ask, "Will it be long until we get to Springbrook?" or "Are we almost there now?"

"In a little while," she answered over and over again. "In just a little while."

Finally it was time to brush hair and straighten jackets.

Belle smiled shyly. "Miss Kelly, the ribbon you gave me got lost somewhere."

"Belle loses everything," Jessie piped up.

"Do not."

"Do too."

"We have more ribbons," Frances said. She handed one to Belle, then retied the drooping bow in Daisy's hair.

Frances glanced over at Aggie. "Would you like a ribbon, Aggie? I've got a lovely white ribbon that would match the collar on your dress."

Aggie shook her head angrily. "I don't need a ribbon. Are people going to want me just because I'm wearing a ribbon?"

"Miss Kelly wants to make your hair look better," Jessie said, "although I don't think anything will help."

Aggie would have fit into Sheriff Malloy's storm prediction. Her eyebrows dipped in a scowl, and her cheeks turned red.

Frances put an arm around Aggie's shoulders. As she smoothed Aggie's skirts, she skillfully turned her so that her back was to Jessie. "You look perfectly lovely," she said.

Aggie's anger hadn't abated. "People aren't supposed to want to adopt me because of what I'm like on the outside. They're supposed to care about what's on the *inside*. They're supposed to care about *me!*"

Frances looked deeply into Aggie's eyes. "You're

right," she said, "and that's the way *you're* supposed to care about *them*."

Flustered, Aggie took a step backward. The anger had disappeared, replaced by confusion.

Maybe I've given her a new direction to think about, Frances thought hopefully.

The conductor strode through the car. "Springbrook, next stop. Springbrook, five minutes."

Frances made sure all their baggage was piled by the door, and as soon as the train stopped, she led the children to the platform.

As before, a number of people were clustered on the platform, waiting for the children to arrive. A tall, thin woman stepped forward and thrust out her hand. "Miss Kelly? I'm Isabelle Domain, chairman of the placing-out committee," she said. "The train will be here in Springbrook for half an hour, so we'll do the choosing right here and now on the platform and get the waifs no one wants back on board."

The waifs no one wants? Frances winced at Mrs. Domain's words and the hardness in her voice, but before she could speak, Mrs. Domain said, "I—that is, *we*—can vouch for everybody who's come to see the children."

Taken aback by Mrs. Domain's rushed manner, Frances said, "But the children and the potential foster parents must have time to get to know one another."

"Hummph!" Mrs. Domain said. "The longer things take, the less gets done. Line up the children, please, and introduce them. We'd better get started."

Frances, realizing she had no other choice, took the children by their hands and placed them with their backs to the train, facing the adults who had gathered.

Smiling, she rested her hands on the shoulders of George and Earl Babcock. "George and Earl are brothers," she said. "They want very much to be placed together."

She moved to Harry and his little brother, Adam, who had wrapped his arms around Harry's waist and clung to him in terror. "Harry and Adam are brothers, too, and they're also hoping for a family who'll take both of them."

She introduced Belle, Daisy, Lucy, Aggie, and Jessie; Jack, Eddie, and Shane; and once again—although Mrs. Domain fussed impatiently—Frances gave her short speech about the Children's Aid Society and what the foster parents must promise to do in raising the children.

Frances stood back, allowing the adults to talk with the children. In the shade at one side of the depot, she caught a glimpse of the man she had seen on the train. This time his hat was pulled low to shade his eyes from the sun, so it wasn't possible to see his face. He was watching her, Frances knew. Why? He couldn't be Seth. He was too short, wasn't he? Or did the distance create that illusion? *He's not Seth*, she told herself firmly.

Eddie stood nearby. He had picked up three stones and was unsuccessfully trying to juggle them and smile at the people around him at the same time. "Learned to juggle on the streets of New York, I did," Eddie said. "Maybe you'd like to hear me whistle a cheery tune while I juggle."

A woman who'd stopped to watch him turned to her husband. " 'Fraid this one's a little smart aleck," she said. "Let's talk to that boy over there."

Eddie dropped the stones, and as he picked them

up, Frances said in a low voice, "Eddie, take a look at the man leaning against the depot."

Eddie straightened and stepped back to look. "What man?" he asked.

Frances stared at the building. The man who looked like Seth was now outside the door to the depot, where Frances could get a closer look. He definitely wasn't Seth. "Never mind," Frances told Eddie. "I made a mistake." Ready to tend to business, she turned back to the people who had stopped to talk to the children.

A man and woman came to Frances, leading George and Earl Babcock by the hand. "The boys said they'd like to come with us," the man said, and introduced himself and his wife.

"They've got four dogs!" Earl exclaimed. "And one of them just had pups! They said one of the pups could be mine!"

"There'll be a pup for each of you," the woman said, beaming. "They're fine boys," she told Frances.

"Yes, they are," Frances agreed, but she could see the depths of sorrow in George's eyes. As eldest brother, he had tried to keep his family together. He'd have his brother with him, but he'd always dream of the little sister he might never see again.

Jack Greer went to a young couple who smiled readily and often, and Daisy Gordon agreed to go with a stout middle-aged couple who told her a happy child brightened a lonely house.

Frances felt at ease about these placements, but she was concerned about the man who asked for Lucy Griggs. Quiet and solemn-faced, he seemed to be as shy as Lucy.

Without introducing himself, he blurted out to Lucy, "My wife sent me to bring home a girl to be a companion to our own little girl. Would you like to come with me?"

Frances asked, "Where is your wife? I'd like to meet her, Mr. . . ."

"Snapes. Wilbur Snapes. Mabel couldn't come. She had to stay home to take care of the child."

"I'm not sure that—" Frances began, but Lucy, tightly clutching her doll, burst into the conversation.

"They have a little girl!" she said. "I'd have a little sister! This is what I wanted right from the beginning!" She looked up at Mr. Snapes. "What's her name?"

"Emma," he answered.

"Emma! That's a lovely name!"

Mrs. Domain stepped up and nodded to Mr. Snapes. "Morning, Wilbur," she said before she turned to Frances. "The Snapes are good-hearted people. I recommend them."

"We usually meet *both* prospective parents," Frances said, but Mrs. Domain shook her head.

"Poor Mabel doesn't get out much, what with Emma to care for, but she's a fine, upstanding woman. Did I mention that Wilbur's a deacon in our church?"

Frances took Lucy aside. "Are you sure you want to live with the Snapeses?" she asked. "You have a choice."

Lucy's eyes sparkled. "I choose *yes*. Miss Kelly, I'm going to have a little sister! I'll share my doll with Emma. Maybe she has a doll, too. Maybe Emma will sit on my lap and I can rock her."

Frances smiled at Lucy. "All right. We'll give Mr. Snapes the papers to sign."

Sudden loud voices nearby caused Frances to

whirl around. Aggie was glowering at the woman who stood before her.

"Open your mouth, child. Let's have a look at your teeth," the woman ordered.

"No! I am not a horse!" Aggie snapped.

The woman's husband scowled at Aggie and took a step toward her. "There'll be no talk like that," he growled.

Aggie looked frightened, but she spoke up. "Don't you dare hit me," she said, "or I'll yell and scream and hit you back."

Frances hurried to Aggie's side and put a protective arm around her shoulders.

"There seems to be a problem here," Frances said, but the woman drew her shawl around her shoulders and stomped off in a huff.

"We don't want the likes of that young savage," her husband said as he followed her.

"I'm not a young savage," Aggie murmured to Frances. "I'm a person. I'm Aggie. And all I want is to be part of a family until . . ."

"What do you mean by *until*?" Frances asked.

Aggie's voice was barely a whisper. "My mother left me on the steps of a hospital when I was born." Defiantly she added, "She had to! She didn't want to leave me!"

"Of course she didn't," Frances said. She held Aggie's hands.

"She wrote a note. She pinned it to my blanket. I have it. I found it in my file in Mrs. Marchlander's office, and I took it, because it belongs to me, not her. My mother wrote that she was in temporary distress—those are the exact words. And she wrote that she would come back for me someday."

"Oh, Aggie, love," Frances said, aching for her.

136

"It's been twelve years," Aggie said, "so I don't think she will." Quickly she corrected herself. "Or can. That's it. She probably can't come. But she loved me, so maybe . . . My mother loved me, and somebody else will. Won't they?"

"Of course they will," Frances said. She spoke to three or four young couples, praising Aggie, but they all shook their heads and drifted away.

Belle Dansing found a home with kind, smiling people, and Frances rejoiced. The little girl who had known nothing but life in an orphanage would now have the parents and love she needed so badly.

Shane Prescott was chosen by people Frances liked immediately. Mrs. Domain gave them high praise.

But soon the people who had come to see the children just out of curiosity drifted away. There were only a few couples left on the platform. Not nearly enough for the children who hadn't been chosen. Frances looked at the worried young faces and felt heartsick.

Mrs. Domain pointedly looked at her watch and announced, "It's a few minutes early, Miss Kelly, but you might as well get the rest of the waifs back on the train."

A young woman bustled up to Frances, a disappointed look on her face. "I'm Annette Sebring," she said. "My husband and I have a farm not far from here. We've been married only four years, and we're doing well, but not well enough to support more than one child."

She stopped as though waiting for Frances to speak, but Frances was puzzled. "We have a number of children here who haven't been chosen yet," she said.

137

"Oh, I know, I know," Mrs. Sebring said. "I guess I'm so concerned about my problem that I didn't make myself clear. There's a darling little boy over there named Adam Stowe, and my husband and I have our hearts set on him. But he said he can't leave his brother. My husband and I talked it over, but we don't see how we can manage to support more than one child."

Frances's heart ached. "Adam and Harry are very close. They've been terribly afraid that they'll be separated."

"But you *do* separate children in families, don't you?" Mrs. Sebring pleaded. "We want Adam, and we'll love him with all our hearts."

"I'll talk to the boys," Frances told her.

"Make it quick," Mrs. Domain said. "The train will leave in five minutes."

Frances knelt in front of Adam and took his tear-stained face in her hands. "Adam, love," she said, "Mr. and Mrs. Sebring want you very much. They'll be good parents to you."

"No," Adam insisted. "I have to stay with Harry."

Frances looked up at Harry. "You understand, don't you? There's just one more stop. It's going to be very hard, if not impossible, to place you together."

Harry nodded, but his face was white with fear. Frances could see the struggle within him as he said, "Adam, you have to go."

"No!"

"They're nice people. I can tell. You'll have a real mother and father again."

"I want our own mother and father."

"You can't. They died. You know that," Harry said.

Adam buried his head against Harry's chest and sobbed.

Harry didn't waver. "You've always done everything I told you to, right?" As Adam nodded, Harry went on. "I want you to go with the Sebrings. You'll be happy with them."

Adam looked up. "But I'll never see you again."

"Yes, you will. We'll write to each other, and maybe, when we're bigger . . ."

"I can't write."

"You'll go to school and learn how. Just remember, someday I'll come and see you. I promise."

Mrs. Domain leaned out of the open window of the railway car and shouted, "Miss Kelly. I've put the children on board. You have only a few minutes left!"

Frances stood and held out her hands to Adam and Harry. "Adam, we have to get the papers signed. Harry, say a quick goodbye to your brother and hop aboard the train."

It took just a few minutes to get the Sebrings' signatures. Frances hadn't realized she'd been crying, too, until Mrs. Sebring handed her a small, lace-trimmed handkerchief.

"Thank you, thank you, thank you, for our boy," Mrs. Sebring whispered. "We'll make him happy."

With the help of the conductor, who held out a hand, Frances boarded the train just as it began to move. Quickly she wiped her eyes. Only four children were left in her care: Harry Stowe, Jessie Lester, Aggie Vaughn, and Eddie Marsh. They sat quietly, wrapped in their own blankets of misery and self-doubt. Reddened eyes and streaked faces showed that they'd been crying—except for Aggie, who sat stubbornly, her lower lip pushed out and her arms folded tightly across her chest.

Aggie had told Frances, "I never cry." Frances wished she could say, "Go ahead and cry. Let all that

139

unhappiness out." But she knew that headstrong Aggie wouldn't listen.

Eddie's laugh was wobbly as he said, "I guess there's not much interest out here in the West for a lad from the big city."

"The right person will come along," Frances said. "It's going to be someone who'll really appreciate all your fine qualities."

"What fine qualities?" Jessie asked. "I heard someone say that Eddie was a smart aleck."

"I just tried to make people laugh," Eddie explained.

Frances patted his hand and smiled. "I liked your juggling act," she said.

Aggie slumped in her seat, her arms folded tightly across her chest, her face a small thundercloud. "I am *not* going back to Mrs. Marchlander," she muttered.

"Of course you're not," Frances said. "I'm sure that there's someone in Woodridge who'll choose you and love you."

"You can't really know for sure," Jessie said. "You're just guessing."

Aggie scowled at Jessie, then turned to Frances. "I'm not going back," she said. "I'll run away first."

"I'll find a home for you—for all of you," Frances promised. She sighed. From the glum expressions on Aggie's and Jessie's faces, it was obvious that she hadn't been able to influence either of them. She hadn't been able to influence Seth. And Johnny? Would she be a failure with Johnny, too?

15

JESSIE TUGGED AT Frances's arm. "No one's going to want us," she said.

Frances patted Jessie's cheek and smiled. "Jessie, love, don't always look at the gloomy side," she said. "Each train makes three stops, and children are chosen at each of the stops."

Jessie looked more mournful than before. "Even the waifs, like us?"

Sighing, Frances said, "That foolish Mrs. Domain was rude and stupid to talk about children in the way she did. Each of you is special and wonderful and deserves a happy home."

"*If* someone chooses us."

Frances slowly shook her head as her gaze went from Jessica, to Harry, to Aggie, and last to Eddie. "Look at these sad faces," she said. "It's a short ride to Woodridge and your new parents. I'd expect you to be excited and impatient."

Harry lifted a somber, tear-swollen face to Frances. "I don't care what happens to me, now that I've lost Adam," he said.

Frances rummaged through her reticule and pulled out a slip of paper. "Here. I've copied down the name and address of the people who took Adam to live with them," she said. "I promised you that I'd give it to you so that you could write to Adam."

Harry grabbed the paper and stuffed it into his pocket. "But the train keeps pulling us farther and farther apart. I won't be able to see Adam in school, or walk to the Sebrings' farm to visit him, or let him know I'm still around to be his big brother and watch over him."

"I understand how you feel," Frances said. "I was parted from my brothers and sisters when we rode the train west, but we wrote to each other and stayed close through our love for each other."

She reached out to hold Harry's hand, but he jerked it away. She didn't blame him for his anger. All the adults who were involved in separating Harry from his little brother had become the enemy. *But I had to follow the rules*, Frances reminded herself. *I couldn't deny a child to the Sebrings and take the chance that someone at the third stop would want two boys.*

Hope shone in Eddie's eyes as he said to Frances, "I've never been a farmer, but I know a pig from a cow, and I'm quick to learn. I'm not afraid of hard work, either. Maybe you could tell 'em that."

"I'm going to brag about all of you," Frances said.

Jessie sniffed. "Eddie does enough bragging about himself."

As the train slowed, Frances straightened a collar, brushed down a jacket, and smoothed back locks of hair. "You all look wonderful," she said.

The train came to a stop and Frances began to collect their baggage, but Aggie interrupted her, gripping Frances's arm with damp fingers. "Please," she begged in a hoarse whisper, "may I have a hair ribbon?"

"Of course," Frances said, and hugged her. She pulled a ribbon from her carpetbag and tied it around Aggie's hair. "You look lovely," Frances said, "and—remember—you're also lovely on the inside, Aggie."

Aggie didn't answer. Her face was pale with fear.

Frances led the children to the station platform, where she was met by a tall, prosperous-looking gentleman who introduced himself. "I'm Arthur Knowles, bank president and chairman of the local committee to approve or disapprove those who apply to adopt the orphan train children."

His eyebrows rose and dipped again. "Only four children? We were hoping for more. There are at least a dozen couples who've come to the schoolhouse to meet the children."

Frances smiled at her charges, but only Eddie smiled back. "Let's not keep them waiting," she said.

She took a step forward, following Mr. Knowles, but stumbled as, in the distance, she saw the man she had thought was Seth. He was standing at the far end of the railway platform, one hand on his horse's reins, facing Frances, but his hat was pulled down, shading his face so that Frances couldn't make out his features.

She gripped Eddie's shoulder and asked, "Who is that man at the far end of the station—the one with the horse?"

"Can't see him," Eddie answered. "Only his pants and boots."

Frances looked up quickly, but the man had moved to the other side of his horse.

If he's Seth, Frances thought, *he's trying to frighten me. But he's not Seth. He can't be. Seth has better things to do than follow me. And didn't Sheriff Malloy tell me that the sheriffs along the route would keep a lookout for Seth?*

The man turned and squinted up at the sun as though trying to tell the time, and Frances could clearly see that he was not Seth. She let out such a long sigh of relief that Mr. Knowles turned to her with a questioning look. *I have to stop worrying about Seth and what he might do,* Frances scolded herself.

"Are you coming, Miss Kelly?" Mr. Knowles asked. "Is anything wrong?"

"Nothing's wrong," Frances said. Standing tall, she strode after Mr. Knowles and the children in her care. All she had time to think of now was finding homes for the four of them.

As they entered the cool dimness of Woodridge's school for the first through the eighth grade, Frances could hear a hum of voices.

"We built the meeting hall along with the school," Mr. Knowles said proudly. "It's the only school in these parts with its own auditorium."

Frances murmured something polite, but her mind was on the people who had stopped talking and had turned to watch as she escorted the children to the stage.

144

She began to speak about the Children's Aid Society's placing-out program. Then, when she introduced the children, she mentioned not only their names and ages, but all the good things she'd observed about them.

"I'll be down here," Frances told them as she left the stage. "Please feel free to talk to the children. I know that you'll love them when you meet them."

Two couples, disappointed expressions on their faces, came to Frances.

"We were hoping for a baby," one woman said.

"We wanted a little boy, around four or five—the age of our only son. These are all older children," another woman complained.

"Jessie is only nine," Frances said. "She's hoping for a mother and father to love."

The woman's husband shook his head. "Too old," he said, and both couples left the auditorium.

But the man and woman who'd been talking to Harry came to Frances. "Harry Stowe's a nice boy," the man said. He held out his hand. "I'm Luther Dunkling, and this is my missus, Rhoda. We'd like to take Harry to live with us."

Frances liked the honest happiness in the Dunklings' faces. She beamed. "Harry is a wonderful boy," she said. "He's going to be sad for a while because his little brother was adopted at the last stop, but please be patient with him. I'm sure he'll be obedient and cooperative and will soon be very happy with you."

Mrs. Dunkling nodded. "I know what to do with unhappy boys," she said. "Give them a lot of love."

Mr. Knowles gave his approval of the Dunklings, and Frances helped them fill out the proper papers.

She hugged Harry, wiping away some of his tears, but he stiffened, and she could feel his anger.

"Harry," Frances whispered, "the Dunklings are good people. They'll be good to you and make you happy."

"How can I be happy without Adam?" Harry said, but he allowed Mr. Dunkling to take his hand as they left the building.

Another couple stepped up. The man was plump, with rosy cheeks and deep laugh lines in his face. His wife was tall and thin and looked as if she rarely smiled.

"We're Ethel and Carl Oliver," the woman said. "We've been approved by the committee—just ask Arthur Knowles. Everything's in order, and we'd like to sign up to take Jessie with us."

Frances glanced at Mr. Knowles, who smiled and nodded. Frances suddenly remembered what Sheriff Malloy's wife had said about committee members approving their best customers or best friends without question, even though they might not be the most satisfactory parents.

Mrs. Oliver kept a steady gaze on Frances. "Could we please sign the papers now? We have a long ride back to our farm."

"I have some questions first," Frances said. "Do you have other children?"

"I gave birth to five. Two survived childhood. They're grown and off on their own."

"What is the purpose in taking Jessie?"

Mrs. Oliver bristled, but Mr. Oliver chuckled. "Our house is too quiet. We'd like to have a child in the house," he said.

Frances took Jessie aside. "Do you want to go

with the Olivers?" she asked. "You have the choice to go or not."

Jessie looked around the room. "I'd say I didn't have much of a choice. This is the third stop and no one's wanted me until now."

"I promise you, Jessie, I'll find a family who'll make you happy," Frances said.

Jessie shrugged. "The Olivers are all right. She's down in the mouth, but he laughs a lot. I'd just as soon know I'll have a home than have to go through all this again."

Frances made sure the papers were in order and watched Jessie—still solemn-faced—being led away.

Only a few people were left in the room when an elderly couple entered. They paused, glanced around, then made their way directly to Aggie.

The woman was arthritic and walked slowly and carefully, the man's hand under her elbow to steady her. They smiled at Aggie, and Frances sighed with relief. Their smiles were warm and their eyes were kind. Frances hurried to join them.

"We're Bertha and Eldon Bradon," the man said.

"We're so glad you're here," Mrs. Bradon said to Aggie. "We wanted a girl."

Aggie's mouth fell open in surprise. She struggled to compose herself and said, "You want *me*?"

"What's your name, child?" Mr. Bradon asked.

"Aggie. That is, it's Agatha Mae Vaughn," Aggie answered.

"A beautiful name," Mr. Bradon said.

"We live less than a mile from this school, Aggie," Mrs. Bradon told her, "and we've always felt that learning is important. So come late September, after the harvest, when school starts up again, you'll be enrolled. How do you feel about going to school?"

"I like to read, and I'm good with my numbers," Aggie answered.

Mr. Bradon's eyes twinkled. "I knew you would be," he said. "I could tell right off you were smart."

Frances saw the corners of Aggie's lips turn down as she glanced at Mrs. Bradon's twisted fingers. "I know why you want me. It's to do your household chores," she said bluntly.

Mrs. Bradon looked surprised. "Only your share, dear. In a family, everyone helps," she said.

Aggie looked from Mrs. Bradon to Mr. Bradon and back again. Seemingly embarrassed by her outburst, she said, "I do want to help around the house, and I'm good at sewing, too."

"Will you come with us and be our little girl?" Mrs. Bradon asked.

Aggie threw a quick, desperate glance at Frances. Frances knew that Aggie had been hoping for young parents to love her. Frances smiled and nodded at Aggie, hoping she'd get the message. There was no rule that parents had to be young. The Bradons were kind, loving people.

Aggie glanced around the nearly empty room and then at Eddie, who sat alone on one side of the stage. "I'll come with you," she said.

After arrangements had been made with the Bradons, Aggie surprised Frances by impulsively wrapping her in a goodbye hug.

"You said someone would come to check on me," she whispered.

"Andrew MacNair will," Frances said.

"Promise?"

148

"I promise," Frances murmured against Aggie's cheek. "But I'm sure you'll want to stay with the Bradons. I have a feeling that you'll be happy with them, Aggie."

Aggie straightened and took a deep breath. "At least I was chosen by people who wanted me. Mrs. Marchlander was wrong."

Frances's heart swelled with pride as she watched Aggie and the Bradons head for the doors. She knew now that Aggie would have a chance to be truly happy.

As soon as Aggie and the Bradons had left, Frances hurried over to Eddie. He jumped off his stool and then off the stage, threw his arms around Frances, and burst into tears.

"I can't go back to New York," he sobbed. "Please, please don't send me back!"

"No one's going to send you back," Frances said. "I promise."

Eddie buried his head against Frances's shoulder. "You promised that someone would want me. You promised I'd have parents and a home."

With one arm Frances held Eddie tightly. With the other hand she reached up to wipe tears from her own eyes. Eddie, with his glib tongue and mischief written all over his face, might have put off people who wanted a dutiful, well-behaved boy; but Frances loved Eddie just the way he was. He reminded her so much of Mike.

Eddie pulled back and looked up into Frances's eyes. "Why don't *you* take me?" he asked. "It don't matter to me that you're not married and I won't have a father. You'll need me all the more because I'll be a big help with the chores. I'm healthy. I'm strong.

149

Sure, I may be small for my age, but who cares? I can do a man's work easy."

"Eddie, there are rules," Frances tried to explain. "The Society believes that the children placed should have both mothers and fathers."

"You work for them," Eddie said, fear in his eyes. "Maybe you could talk to someone who owes you a favor."

Frances sat on the edge of the stage and took his hands. "That's not the way I do things, Eddie," she said. "And I'm sure the people in the Children's Aid Society don't either. But there *is* something I can do."

"What?" Eddie's voice had dropped to a whisper.

"My mother lives in St. Joe," Frances said. "Let's pay her a visit. She's full of good ideas." Frances grinned. "And advice, too. And while we're there, we can talk to Andrew MacNair. He's the agent in charge. Between us we'll find you a happy home."

She stood and walked over to Mr. Knowles. "Do you know when the next train to St. Joe comes through?"

He looked at his watch. "Not until four o'clock, but as you know, it's a short trip—less than an hour." He looked at Eddie. "I didn't know that St. Joe was a scheduled stop for the orphan train riders."

"It isn't," Frances said. "My mother lives in St. Joe, and I'd like to spend a few days with her."

Mr. Knowles nodded. "We'll finish the paperwork, and I'll see that the two of you get a good dinner. Then I'll take you to the depot." Under his breath he said to Frances, "Do you think you'll find a home for the lad?"

"I *know* I will," Frances said, but her heart gave a thump. Three groups of people had been unable to see Eddie's special qualities—his good humor, high-spiritedness, and quickness of mind—the very qualities she treasured in her brother Mike. However, she *would* find a good home for Eddie. She had to. The promise she had made had not been just to Eddie. It had been to herself.

16

MA WAS OVERJOYED to see Frances and welcomed Eddie by leading him to the kitchen. "You're a handsome lad," Ma said, "but far too thin for your own good. Someone's going to have to put some meat on those bones." She smiled down at Eddie. "You remind me of my son Mike. Same red hair, same mischievous look, same big smile."

Eddie beamed and lit into the beef stew that Ma had heated up and served to them.

"Can you keep Eddie a few days, until Andrew and I find him a home?" Frances asked.

"Of course I can," Ma assured her. "And I can tell you right now, it'll be fine with John as well."

"I wish I could adopt him," Frances said quietly to her mother. "Eddie and I have shared a lot, and I feel so close to him." She sighed. "In a way I'm going to be jealous of whoever gets him."

"Why can't you adopt Eddie?" Ma asked.

"There are rules. No single parents."

Ma just raised an eyebrow. She had no time to say what she meant because Peg bounced into the room.

Peg greeted Eddie quickly, then flew into her sister's arms. "Why are you here, Frances? Where have you been? Tell me! Tell me everything!" she cried.

Frances settled into one of the comfortable overstuffed chairs in the living room and told Ma and Peg why she had gone to New York and about the orphan train children and their trip to Missouri.

"The building we lived in is gone, you say," Ma murmured, and Frances could see memories pile like tears in her mother's eyes.

"But the church was still there," Frances told her, "and it looked exactly as it did when we lived on Sixteenth Street."

Ma's fingers plucked at the edge of the tablecloth. "That seems like such a long time ago."

Frances grinned, leaning forward. "I saw Mr. Lomax," she said, and went on to tell how she had puzzled him by speaking to him.

Ma laughed with delight. "So your journey both ways was uneventful," she said. "I'm glad of that."

Eddie smothered a noise, and Frances glanced at him, her eyes twinkling. There was a flash of humor in Eddie's eyes, but it was obvious that he was a very tired boy.

"Ma, can we make up a bed for Eddie?" Frances asked.

"After a good hot bath," Ma suggested, but Frances shook her head.

"Sleep first, bath tomorrow. Eddie's had a very tiring day."

Peg jumped to her feet. "I'll put sheets on the bed in the spare room for Eddie," she said. "Frances can sleep with me."

As Peg and Eddie left the room, Ma said, "Frances, I'd like to hear more about the children you brought to new homes."

"I wrote about all thirty children in the last few pages of my journal," Frances said. She put the blue cloth-bound book on the table and said, "Wait until I make us some tea. Then I'll use the journal to refresh my memory."

She found some gingerbread in the pantry and arranged pieces on a plate while she waited for the water in the kettle to come to a boil. Finally the tea had steeped in the pot long enough to have body, and Frances carried the tray with the teapot, cups, plates, and gingerbread into the living room.

Ma waited until Frances had poured the tea, then said, "I was impatient. I glanced through the journal."

"Ma!" Frances said.

"You didn't tell me it was a private journal," Ma said. "I thought you had written about the children in your care."

"I did."

Ma shrugged. "A little." She looked stern. "You didn't tell me about that man named Seth and what happened on the train. Just who was this Seth?"

Frances sighed. "As you probably read, I met Seth on the orphan train in the New Jersey depot. He was disguised as a preacher to escape the police, but he is a former Confederate soldier. A poor, mixed-up man who's filled with hatred and bitterness about the war, like . . . like . . ."

"Like Johnny? You wrote quite a bit about Johnny."

"Oh, Ma!" Frances said. "Johnny is never going to ask me to marry him. He even refuses to discuss marriage. He broods about the Confederate prison camp and what the Rebs did, and he's shut me out completely." She rested her head in her hands and said, "I thought I could forget about him, but I can't. I love him too much."

"Then don't give up," Ma said.

Frances looked down, blushing. "We had a terrible argument. There were things I said . . ."

"There are words to undo the harm. Try."

"How?"

"Send Johnny a letter. Tell him when you'll return to Maxville. Tell him you missed him."

"What if I don't hear from him?"

"You'll never know if you don't try."

Frances thought a moment. "But I don't know when I'll go back. I'll have to find a good home for Eddie first. He's a special boy, Ma. I care very much what happens to him."

Ma smiled and reached over to squeeze Frances's hand. "Oh, Frances, love," she said, "I thought you would have figured out the answer to that one by this time."

17

THE NEXT MORNING Frances wrote to Johnny. Then, with Eddie at her side, she walked to town to mail the letter. "Let's take a side trip on our way to the post office," she said. "I want you to get a glimpse of the Missouri River in sunlight."

The path Frances chose cut through a wooded area. When she and Eddie were deep in the shadow of the trees she thought she heard footsteps and the *clip-clop* of a horse's hooves. She stopped and listened, but there were no sounds at all, not even the usual trills of the birds.

Was it my imagination? she asked herself. Eddie was laughing and scurrying after a rabbit. Surely he would have heard the footsteps, if they had been real. Frances walked on, Eddie darting here and there to examine new things.

Again she heard the footsteps and the hoofbeats. She stopped and turned. Taking a deep breath to steady herself, she said, "Come out, Seth. Talk to me. I won't harm you."

Eddie, eyes frightened, dashed to Frances's side.

For a long moment there was nothing but silence. Then a horse whinnied, and Seth walked out from behind a thick stand of trees and brush, leading his horse. He wore his flat-brimmed black hat and Confederate jacket.

"Oh, Seth," Frances said sadly, "why did you come after me?"

He came closer, one hand on the butt of the gun he had stuck into his belt. His face was hard, his mouth pressed into a thin, angry line as he glared at her. "I wanted you to know what it felt like to be tracked . . . to be hunted, as if you were no better than an animal. I told you I'd find you, wherever you were, didn't I?"

Afraid of choosing the wrong words, Frances didn't answer.

Finally Seth said, "You turned in my brothers and me. I didn't think you'd do that. I never would have believed you could do a thing like that. You're going to have to pay, Frances."

Frances clutched the reins, pressing her trembling fingers into the folds of her skirt as she fought to stay calm. "You robbed those people on the train," she answered. "And you were going to rob a bank. You planned to steal money from innocent people. Some of them wouldn't be able to replace their savings."

Seth shrugged. "Why should I worry about people I don't even know? When I was in trouble did they do anythin' for me?"

"How could they?" Frances asked. "They had no control over what our armies did." Eddie squirmed, and Frances pressed one hand against his shoulder, warning him to be silent.

"Someone has to give instead of take. Someone has to care," Frances told Seth. "You want someone to care about you."

"Nobody cares about me, except my brothers," Seth grumbled. "And that's the way I like it." His face twisted in pain. "I had hopes about you, but . . ."

His eyes on Frances, Seth slowly pulled his gun from his belt. "You turned me in," he said. "You shouldn't have done it. I got away, but my brothers are in jail."

Frances, terrified, tried not to stare at the gun. "Seth," she asked, "what good will it do to kill me?"

"You know," he said. "It's justice. It's my way of gettin' justice."

"Lawlessness isn't justice. Getting even doesn't solve anything."

Seth didn't answer, so Frances—desperately hoping that he'd listen to reason—went on. "You told me you wanted to get revenge for what happened to your parents. Suppose your mother and father were standing here with us. They loved you. They cared about you. Do you think they'd want to see you shoot me because of some mixed-up notion you have about making things come out even?"

"You've got no right to talk about my parents!" Seth shouted.

"Sometimes I think about my own parents and the hopes they might have had for me. You'll go to jail if you kill me. Your parents wouldn't have wanted to see you in jail. Your parents wouldn't have wanted you to become a murderer just to get revenge," Frances told him.

"Be quiet," Seth ordered. But there was a catch in his voice.

"I know you were good to your mother, and she was proud of you. And your father respected your courage in going off to fight for what you believed in, and—"

Seth, his eyes wet with tears, jabbed his handgun into his belt and yelled, "I wish I'd never met you, Frances Kelly!"

He leaped onto his horse, jerked at the reins, and kicked with his spurs. The horse leaped forward, eyes rolling, and shot off through the trees.

As Seth disappeared from sight, Eddie leaned against Frances and said, "I thought we were done for."

"So did I," Frances admitted.

"Do you think he'll come back?"

"No," Frances said. "I don't think he will." She hugged Eddie in relief, then gave in to her tears as she shook with fear at what might have happened.

Finally Frances hunted through the pockets of her skirt and came up with the wrinkled lace-trimmed handkerchief Mrs. Sebring had given her.

"You were great," Eddie told her. "You said Seth had courage, but so do you."

Frances thought about the children who had just been placed, who had walked away, hand in hand with strangers, to begin new lives. "So do we *all*," she said, and managed to smile at Eddie.

Frances and Eddie walked rapidly the rest of the way to town, stopping first at the post office to buy a stamp and mail Frances's letter to Johnny. Frances allowed a three-day wait until her arrival. That would give him time to think . . . to decide. . . .

Her letter had been short and to the point:

Dearest Johnny . . . I'm sorry for what I said and the hurt I caused you. I've missed you terribly. I want to see you, and I'm hoping you'll want to see me. I'll arrive by train in Maxville at two in the afternoon on Thursday, August tenth. . . .

With my love, Frances

Was Ma right? Would these be healing words?

Eddie tugged at her arm, pulling her back, as she attempted to step off the wooden sidewalk. "Miss Kelly!" he shouted. "Watch where you're going! You nearly stepped in front of that dray!"

Shaken, Frances said, "I'm sorry, Eddie. My mind's not on what I'm doing."

He nodded, solemn for a change. "You're worried about me, aren't you? Well, don't be. Whatever happens to me, I can handle it. I always have. I always will."

Frances rested a hand on his shoulder. "Don't look so unhappy. You'll have a home. Didn't I promise you?" she said. "Right now I want you to meet the Children's Aid Society agent, Andrew MacNair."

As soon as there was a break in the traffic, Frances said, "Come on, Eddie. Hurry!" She lifted her skirts from the dust and strode across the street, nimbly avoiding the horse and ox droppings. Once on the sidewalk she said, "Andrew has an office in the back of his wife's general store. We'll see if he's there."

Katherine MacNair had seen Frances coming and waited for her inside the store. Wrapped in Katherine's hug, Frances reveled in the mixed fragrances of cinnamon sticks and peppermint, newly picked peaches piled in a display, and tart dill pickles, bobbing in a barrel of tangy brine.

Holding Frances at arm's length so that she could study her face, Katherine asked, "You're looking well. Prettier than ever. How was the trip? Did the children behave? Did all of them find homes?"

Andrew MacNair stepped up behind his wife and laughed. "I'm the one to be asking those questions, Katherine. Frances came not just to see your smiling face, but to give me her report."

Frances turned to see Eddie wandering among the counters, studying the array of merchandise for sale. It was just as well he wasn't within earshot. Frances didn't like talking about children over their heads, as though they couldn't hear.

She handed a thick folder of papers to Andrew. All the children were taken, except one," she said. "Eddie—the young man browsing two counters away. The one with the red hair. I'll call him over and introduce him in just a few minutes."

"My! That's a real mop of red," Katherine said with a smile. "It makes me think of Mike."

Frances nodded. "And, like Mike, Eddie has a lot of the roughness of the New York City streets in him."

Andrew frowned. "Then he'll be hard to place. Offhand, I don't know of anyone who—"

Frances sighed. "I'll find him a good home. He's a wonderful boy, so much like Mike was at his age. Eddie's funny and lovable and smart—"

Katherine interrupted with a laugh. "It sounds as though you're pretty much taken with him yourself."

Shaking her head, Frances said, "You don't need to remind me. No single-parent adoptions." She glanced again at Eddie. "Until a home is found for Eddie, he can stay with Ma and her husband. "Will that be all right with you?"

"Of course," Andrew said. "But I'll need to know as soon as possible if you find a good home for Eddie."

Frances smiled. "Believe me, I'll rush to tell you."

Even though Frances loved the time spent with Ma and Peg and Eddie and John Murphy, the days passed slowly. She couldn't help wondering if Johnny had got her letter, and if so, how he'd received it. He'd been angry, and so had she. Maybe he wouldn't come. . . . Frances shook her head. She wouldn't allow herself to become frightened by what she had done.

But on the train ride to Maxville she couldn't fight the worry any longer. As she thought about arriving at the station, alone, without Johnny there to greet her, her neck and back ached, and the palms of her hands grew damp and clammy.

When the train pulled into the station and came to a stop, Frances peered eagerly from the windows, but there was no sign of Johnny.

Wearily she picked up her carpetbag and carried it down the steps to the depot platform.

"Frances!"

Johnny spoke again from the shadows at the east side of the building. "Frances!"

She ran into his arms and, heedless of the undisguised interest of other passengers, threw her arms around his neck.

"I brought you flowers," he said without loosening his hold. "I'm afraid the midday sun was hard on them, but they're from my heart."

162

"I love them," Frances said. "Oh, Johnny, I love *you!*"

"And I love you."

She was reluctant to leave his embrace, but people were watching and smiling.

"The wagon's over here," Johnny said. He hoisted her carpetbag into the back and helped Frances climb to the wagon seat.

They were silent as they rode through town, but when they reached the open road toward the schoolhouse, Frances said, "There's so much bottled up inside me. There's so much I need to say. To begin with, I'm sorry."

Johnny looked at her, surprised. "Sorry? For what?"

"For my temper, for not understanding," Frances said. She placed a hand on his arm. "I can understand much better now how you feel."

She launched into the story of the train trip, and meeting Seth, and how Eddie knew about the telegraph equipment so that the Connally brothers could be stopped from robbing the bank.

"You're almost as bitter about what happened to you with the Confederates as Seth is about his treatment at the hands of the Union Army—" Frances said.

Johnny interrupted. "You talked about the bitterness before you left. At first your words made me angry, but I've given them a lot of thought and finally came to admit that you were right. But I still have moments of physical weakness . . . nightmares . . . sweats. . . ." His chin stiffened with stubbornness and embarrassment.

"A good wife can also be a good nurse," Frances said.

163

Johnny took her hand. "While you were gone I found out one very important thing," he said. "I can't live without you, Frances. We'll work together as partners, just like you said, but until we have children old enough to share the chores, I'll hire help."

Frances laughed aloud as the idea hit her. Ma had said, "I thought you would have figured out the answer." Even Katherine had seen how much she cared for Eddie. Why had they been able to see what she felt for Eddie when she herself hadn't?

Frances looked up at Johnny and grinned. "How would you like an eleven-year-old son?"

Johnny nearly dropped the reins. "A what?"

"He's an orphan train rider named Eddie Marsh," Frances explained. "No one chose him, but he quickly became my favorite. I'd like to adopt him and give him a home as our son. When he's not in school, he can help with the family chores, as any son would." She paused. "You'll love Eddie, too. He's a tough little kid. He'll remind you of Mike when he was eleven. He needs you to be his father. I need you to be my husband."

For a moment Johnny just shook his head in wonder. Then he grinned at Frances, pulled the horses to a stop, and dropped the reins. "I think, judging from all we've been talking about, it's time that I formally proposed marriage. Will you consent to be my wife, Frances Mary Kelly?"

"Yes, I will," Frances said.

"And you'll bring, as your dowry, an eleven-year-old son?"

Frances laughed with delight and threw her arms around Johnny. "Yes, yes, yes!"

Johnny took a soft cloth from his pocket, unfolded it, and brought out a narrow gold ring. "This

164

was my grandmother's," he said. "My parents and I want you to have it." His eyes twinkled. "I told my parents what I was going to ask you. My mother said she'd pray you'd say *yes.*"

"You have wonderful parents," Frances said, "and they have a wonderful son." Heedless of what might be considered proper, ladylike behavior, she wrapped her arms around Johnny's neck and kissed him soundly.

18

GRANDMA CLOSED THE journal and laid it on the wicker table.

"Oh, Grandma," Jennifer said. "Please don't tell us you've come to the end. There have to be more stories about the Kelly family."

"In any life there are always more stories," Grandma said. "In your own lives you yourselves will keep creating stories. And you will tell your stories to future generations."

Jeff shrugged and shook his head. "Stories about *my* life. I don't think so. What kind of stories could those be?"

Grandma pulled Jeff to his feet and hugged him. "That's entirely up to you," she said.

Jennifer jumped up, too. "Grandma, what about all those orphan train children? Will Aggie be happy?

Will Lucy have that little sister she wants so much? Will Adam and Harry ever get back together again? I want to know!"

"You will," Grandma said. "Each of those orphan train children came up against problems to conquer, and each has a story to tell. Just be patient, my loves, and you'll hear them."

About the Author

JOAN LOWERY NIXON is the acclaimed author of more than a hundred books for young readers. She has served as regional vice-president of the Southwest Chapter of the Mystery Writers of America and is the only four-time winner of the Edgar Allan Poe Best Juvenile Mystery Award given by that society. She is also a two-time winner of the Golden Spur Award, which she won for *A Family Apart* and *In the Face of Danger*, the first and third books of the Orphan Train Adventures. She was moved by the true experiences of the children on the nineteenth-century orphan trains to research and write the Orphan Train Adventures, which also include *Caught in the Act, A Place to Belong, A Dangerous Promise*, and *Keeping Secrets*.

Joan Lowery Nixon and her husband live in Houston, Texas.